THE FORTUNE HUNTER

Could the elegant young lawyer who came so fortuitously into Amy's life really be no more than a fortune-hunter? He alone can defend her father against the murder charges trumped up by the evil men behind the smuggling ring centred on nearby Poole Harbour. With her father locked up in Winchester Goal and her mother distraught, Amy comes to rely more and more on Jeffrey Maldon's advice. When the smugglers catch up with him too, Amy finds herself involved in a terrifying race to outwit the 'Pegmen' in a desperate bid to save the fortune-hunter's life.

The Fortune-Hunter

by
Julia Herbert

MAGNA PRINT BOOKS
Long Preston, North Yorkshire,
England.

British Library Cataloguing in Publication Data.

Herbert, Julia.
    The fortune-hunter.
    I. Title
    823'.914(F)   PR6058.E6/

    ISBN 0-86009-662-9

First Published in Great Britain by Mills & Boon Ltd, 1977

Published in Large Print 1985 by arrangement with Mills & Boon Ltd, London.

Photoset in Great Britain by
Dermar Phototypesetting Co, Long Preston, North Yorkshire.

Printed and bound in Great Britain by
Redwood Burn Limited, Trowbridge, Wiltshire.

CHAPTER ONE

Miss Tyrell was on her knees in the herb garden, harvesting the blossoms of the cinquefoil for the making of a skin lotion, a preparation much in demand among the friends and neighbours who thronged to her father's house. A wide canvas apron protected her taffeta gown; her head was protected from the buffeting sea breeze from the Solent by a straw hat securely tied down with a broad blue ribbon; over her little high-heeled shoes were slippers of bast, woven by the adoring hands of the under-gardener. If young ladies of quality will insist on the actual practice of gardening instead of merely admiring the results, thought Bryce, they must be safeguarded against their own fool-hardiness.

Amy was engrossed in her work. The small basket at her side was half-full of small yellow petals. She wriggled further

7

along the narrow path between the herb beds and stretched for a plant some two feet off; it eluded her because the folds of her skirt caught, behind her, on a shrub.

'Allow me, Miss Tyrell,' said a voice. And a long arm shot out over her shoulder, a hand gathered the flower, and it was deposited in her basket.

Amy, still on her hands and knees, looked round and up.

'Mr. Maldon.' She said the name without enthusiasm.

'Good morning, Miss Tyrell. They told me I should find you here.'

Had they indeed. It was extremely provoking of them to tell him anything of the kind. Did Palmer the butler really imagine she wished to be discovered on her knees on a gritty garden path in gardening gloves and looking a fright? Since it was only Mr. Maldon, it didn't greatly matter. But supposing it had been Bernard?

'Good morning, Mr. Maldon,' she replied, scrambling to her feet with his help. And despite the fact that it was not Bernard, she took off the thick gloves and began to untie the apron.

'I've been sitting for a quarter of an hour with your parents, ma'am, and since you did not come in they were so good as to suggest I might come out.'

Really, Papa was extraordinary! Could he not see what was plain to herself and Mama, that the man was only waiting his opportunity to propose? But no—Papa was all that was good and honest and upright, and could not be expected to notice such small matters as another fortune-hunter. He was too taken up with local affairs, and the troubled policies that had succeeded the Jacobite Rising of '45.

Sometimes Amy doubted that Mr. Maldon was a fortune-hunter. She had seen three or four since she came out, and in general they talked a lot more than Mr. Maldon and, when talking, paid a great many more compliments. Maldon was not precisely taciturn, but he shared a characteristic with her father—he seemed to have little time for empty chatter. In a way, that made his favourable comments all the more valuable—or would have done if Amy's heart had not been already safely lodged with Bernard.

To her it was a mystery why her father seemed positively to encourage Mr. Maldon. He had come to Markledon, a quiet Hampshire market town, practically unknown and with his living to make as a lawyer. He had been settled here not quite three months. For eleven weeks of those three months he had been paying Amy marked attentions. She reflected that since he was tall, well-spoken, and reasonably goodlooking, she might have been in some danger from him even though—on the debit side—he was clearly not rich and probably wanted her money more than her person.

To Amy it was a source of secret amusement that the various young men who had thought to marry into her money were quite unaware how safely she was from them. She was going to marry Bernard—no one else. That was settled, even though it had never been put into words between them. One day ... when Bernard got tired of playing the gay bachelor ... one day ... he would say it: 'I love you, Amy. You must be my wife.'

'I hope I don't interrupt your employment,' Mr. Maldon was saying as he took from her the ugly apron and folded it under his arm. 'But I must confess I'm glad of an opportunity to speak to you alone. With so many friends continually calling at your house, Miss Tyrell, such chances are rare.'

Oh dear, thought Amy. Here it comes.

If she hadn't been taken so much at a disadvantage, she would have tried to turn the conversation to some safe route—for after all, it gave her no pleasure to say no to a man who had hopes of whatever kind, in asking her to marry him.

'I came to take my leave, ma'am,' he went on. 'I am going to London on business for a while.'

Amy had the grace to colour a little. So much for her self-importance! Mr. Maldon had merely come, as politeness required, to take a temporary farewell.

'But before I go,' he said, 'there is something I should like to ask you.'

'Yes, sir?' she said bravely.

'Shall we walk into the shelter of the chestnut trees? I'm sure it's too cool for you in this strong sea breeze.' He offered

11

his arm, and after a momentary hesitation she took it and walked with him. It was best to get it over.

Maldon led her to a smooth stone bench that had acted as bed to many a French doll of hers. Overhead the chestnut trees spread their broad green fingers. She sat down and looked up at him, outlined against the green, and wished he would sit down and look less like a wellbred giant about to eat her.

'What I wish to ask,' he began, after a fractional hesitation, 'is prompted by the general chit-chat of the neighbourhood. You're no doubt aware that your affairs are often talked over by your acquaintance.'

'Lud, yes, sir. I discuss theirs, why shouldn't they discuss mine?'

'And yet, it's sometimes vexing to hear that thoughts of great importance and privacy are the topic of small-talk.' He gazed down at her, his expression grave. 'In short, it is generally supposed by your friends and neighbours that you are engaged to a gentleman of this district. Is it impertinent to ask if they are right?'

'No, sir,' Amy said with some reluc-

_ance, 'if they say I am engaged, they are wrong. If I were, I should let it be known—it wouldn't be a matter for conjecture.'

'Your pardon, Miss Tyrell. I didn't mean to imply anything so reprehensible as a secret engagement.' Maldon's broad hand went up to his plain cravat, and it occurred to Amy that for a fortune-hunter, he was very ill at ease. 'The feeling is that you are ... strongly attached to a gentleman, and as, so far as they can see, the match would please both families, they regard it as likely that you will soon be married.'

'Well, sir?' Amy said, feeling a little prick of resentment against him. Why should he interfere in her affairs? Why should he bring up before her this puzzle that had begun to trouble her greatly— the lack of a declaration from Bernard. 'Was that your question? Whether or not I am engaged? If so, I have answered it.'

'Forgive me, I have expressed myself badly. I needed to know whether your friends were correct in their assumption that you were already promised to another—or if there is any room for me to hope.'

'I can answer the last part for you,' she said with an appearance of composure. 'The answer is no.'

He gave a wry smile. 'From the tone of your voice I take it there was no chance for me in any case, even without the prior claim that your neighbours speak of. I apologise for embarrassing you with my entreaties.'

There was an unexpected note in his voice as he said this; something, she thought, more than the disappointment of a man seeing a wealthy catch elude him. Her resentment melted away. Perhaps, after all, it had not been entirely a matter of finance with him, even though he clearly had little money of his own. Standing there so tall and imposing in his plain blue coat, he had little of the gallant about him; he looked like a man with a great deal of self-control who was taking a hard knock with stoic acceptance.

She was surprised at her surge of sympathy for him. Ever since he had appeared in her circle of acquaintance, she had been using up energy in being rather cool towards Mr. Maldon, even though other young ladies of the district declared him to be the handsomest newcomer Markledon had welcomed in many a long day. Handsome? Was he handsome? For Amy, good looks in a man were always measured by Bernard's fine pale skin and dark eyes. Mr. Maldon, with his fair hair brushed back in a plain bow, his cool grey glance, his sinewy body better suited to the open air than the drawing-room, was almost the opposite of her pattern of masculine attractiveness. Yet at his moment she felt an absurd longing to put a hand upon his arm and feel the firm muscles under his sleeve. She almost wished ... yes, almost, but not quite ... that she had flirted a little with Mr. Maldon. He might have been allowed to steal a kiss—what would it be like, she wondered, to be kissed by Jeffrey Maldon?

Astounded at this errant thought, she pulled herself together.

'You haven't embarrassed me, sir,' she said gently. 'I'm sorry that you should be disappointed, but some other young lady will have the good fortune to make you happy.'

He shook his head. 'That's unlikely. And now, as I can think of nothing in the way of small-talk, I'll make my retreat if you wish to turn back to your gardening.'

'No, the wind as you say is too strong. I believe I shall go indoors, if you will give me your arm.'

He stooped and offered it. As she got to her feet she felt the strength of his muscles under the blue cotton of his summer coat, and found herself wondering what it would be like to have that arm come about her in an embrace … Bernard sometimes hugged her, and that was—oh, delightful, entrancing. But there was something brotherly about it. Whereas if Mr. Maldon were to sweep her into his arms, she sensed that it might be an experience to make the world rock under her feet.

'Shall you be long in London, Mr. Maldon?' she inquired, hurrying into speech to banish these strange thoughts.

'That's uncertain. I have to attend to some complicated matters of business which may take some time, since their completion depends not on myself but on others who may prove dilatory. From

16

what your friends were saying, I gather that on return I may find you married?'

'Oh no, sir,' she exclaimed. Really, people were odd! As if she would be asked for and married within a couple of weeks—! 'No, I must confess to you that although I think of myself as promised, I can't believe I shall be a married woman so soon.'

'In that case I apologise again,' Maldon said, frowning. 'Your friends talked in such a way that I felt I must speak before I left, however slender the chance. Perhaps I'm wrong to report it, but they seem to think you will be married within the month.'

'He has been gambling again,' Amy said with a sigh. 'When he loses money at cards, the gossips always become more active! As if the only way to pay his gambling debts was to marry me—which is absurd!'

Jeffrey Maldon stifled the words that rose up in him, which were to the effect that any man who allowed Miss Tyrell to be spoken of in that way by gossips deserved to be horsewhipped. New in the area, and slow to be accepted by the parochial minds of Markledon, he had had to piece together hints and nods about Amy's situation. Her father was kind enough to invite him quite frequently to the house, and on the occasions when Bernard Gramont was present he had sensed a strong affection flowing out to the man from Amy. But he was less sure that the current flowed the other way.

Incredible though it seemed, Bernard Gramont didn't appear to be in love with Amy.

Well, there are some men who are utter fools, Maldon knew. Men who are given all the gifts of the gods—good looks, charm, money, a family of some influence and, as if that were not enough, the love of the most beautiful and intelligent girl in the world—and yet who seem to want to do nothing with it. Bernard was one such: his mother and sisters adored him, his father had handed on to him the fine features and winning ways that made him the conqueror of all the young ladies in the neighbourhood. Maldon had never been invitd to their home, Parall, but from all accounts it was very handsome inside. Their clothes, their style of living, bespoke money. Certainly Bernard had no need to take Amy for the sake of her fortune.

But to have Amy Tyrell in love with him made him the most fortunate man in the world. Could he not see that she was a nonpareil? That flawless skin, touched with soft warm colour along the cheekbones ... the wide mouth that could curve into a smile impossible to resist ... the trim, upright figure moving elegantly through the minuet at the Assembly Ball, easy to distinguish even in the throng because no other woman carried her head in just that proud way ...

Yet instead of settling down with her, he preferred to racket around with card-players and horse-copers; his exploits were the talk of the coffee-houses.

Perhaps he was just immature. Still sowing his wild oats, as the saying went. All the same, Maldon understood why Mr. Tyrell sometimes looked anxiously at Bernard as he teased Amy. When was the man going to come to the point? How long must his daughter be kept dangling? It was a wonder that the situation had not caused an eruption of Mr. Tyrell's rather unruly temper—but then, where his daughter was concerned, Mr. Tyrell would do almost anything rather than upset her.

Once indoors, Amy and Mr. Maldon found other visitors assembled. Her father, ever anxious to further her cause, had invited the Gramont family to dinner, or at least that part of it that was invitable—only one daughter was "out", Janet, a year or so older than Bernard. She was sitting by her mother, the two of them dark and pretty, although Mrs. Gramont was faded now. It always seemed to Maldon that Mrs. Gramont's looks had drained away as if to enhance her husband's, for he was still one of the handsomest men Maldon had ever seen. "Beau" Gramont, men called him: elegant, dark-eyed, his hair always finely dressed and sparkling with the best imported French powder, his clothes setting off his almost Italianate skin and black brows.

His son Bernard was as good to look upon, perhaps even more so because, darting about the country after entertainment, he spent less time on his appearance. His clothes were more casual than his father's—plainer shoes without diamanté on the buckles, less lace about the throat. Yet such lace as he wore was the finest Point d'Alencon, and the buttons of his waistcoat were skilfully wrought gold.

Mr. Maldon sighed a little to himself. He felt very conscious of some worn edges to his coat, the plainness of his linen. No wonder Miss Tyrell preferred Bernard Gramont ...

Amy had been in love with Bernard for nearly eleven years. She remembered well the first time she ever saw him. The house whose land ran with her father's was called Parall, and it had stood empty for some months. Then there was talk of a new owner, a man with a family, and she had rejoiced at the thought of other children to play with. Aged ten, she had had some lonely days since the Hayhams went away.

Through a gap in the hedge she had watched the travelling coach draw to a halt outside the great porch of Parall, and seen the newcomers alight. Bernard had been first, jumping down with a shout of glee at being free of the stuffy conveyance. Even then he had had that heart-catching charm which never left him. His father had it too. Quick, enthusiastic, a little flamboyant—and irresistible. It was no wonder to Amy that the women of the family were their willing slaves.

Perhaps Bernard would speak today. Perhaps, in the close society of Markledon, some rumour had reached him of Mr. Maldon's interest, and he would be spurred to action. True, two proposals in twenty-four hours were a little too much to hope for, but one day Bernard must speak. One day he would ask her. It had to be so. If not, why was she alive at all?

She greeted the guests; then, with a nod of approval from her father, invited Mr. Maldon to join them. As she went upstairs she wasn't sure whether she was glad or sorry that Mr. Maldon was staying.

Ah well ... he'd be gone soon.

As she passed her mother's room Mrs Tyrell, still dressing, heard her footsteps. 'My dear, come in a moment,' she called. 'What did he say? He seemed very anxious to see you.'

'Who, Mama?' asked Amy, feigning obtuseness.

'Mr. Maldon, of course. What did he say to you? A little bird did tell me it was something very particular.'

'Couldn't the same little bird have given you the particulars?'

'Come, don't be secretive, Amy. What did you say to him? Isn't it strange, my love, fair-haired men always seem to fall in love with you. I remember Mr. Standish, who was so mad after you during the London season—'

'It might be truer to say that the fair-haired Mr. Standish was mad after my money. And in any case, Mr. Maldon's hair is quite a different shade from Mr. Standish's—he wears almost no powder, have you noticed?'

'I notice, dearest, that you are a great deal more aware of Mr. Maldon than you appear,' teased Mrs. Tyrell. 'So I hope you were kind to him?'

'Not unkind, I believe. But he seemed to make up his mind about me so very quickly—almost as soon as he saw me, in fact. One might also say, *before* he saw me—as if he'd come to Markledon on purpose to try for my hand.'

'You don't think Mr. Maldon is a fortune-hunter, do you, my love? Your Papa seems to have a regard for him.'

'I have come to the conclusion that perhaps I misjudged him,' Amy confessed. 'But you know, Mama, even supposing I cared a jot for him, it would be a most imprudent match. He hasn't a penny.'

Mrs. Tyrell smoothed down the front of her gown and waved dismissal at her maid who had been lacing it up at the back. 'As to Mr. Maldon's income, Amy—well, you know, your father could do a good deal for him in his career as a lawyer.'

Amy thought about it. 'I don't think Mr. Maldon is the kind of man who would want his father-in-law to help him in his career,' she ventured. 'But this is all suppositious! You know I don't have to concern myself about Mr. Maldon.'

'No, indeed, there's only one young man we concern ourselves with, isn't there?' Her mother sighed. 'But, Amy,' she went on, 'why does not Bernard propose? I'm sure I've expected your engagement every day since you were eighteen, but nothing comes of it.'

Amy bent her head to conceal the blush of vexation that this thrust produced. 'Well, ma'am, you know Bernard is only a year older than I. Twenty-one is full young for a man to settle.'

'Why, my dear, your father and I were married when he was Bernard's age—aye, married and expecting our family!'

'Yes, but Mama, I think that my father was never like Bernard. Bernard is so— so lively and full of a thousand interests. Papa has always been serious, I imagine.'

'I hope Bernard will prove to be serious,' Mrs. Tyrell said pouting. 'It will be very dreadful if you have refused four offers for his sake, and then he fails you.'

'But, dear madam, you wouldn't have me accept a man—any man, Mr. Maldon for example—simply to avoid being an old maid?'

Mrs. Tyrell laughed. 'You are in no danger, my Amy. Go, take off that hat and cap and get Molly to do your hair with some fresh flowers or perhaps a feather. Give Bernard something to think about—perhaps if he sees you have dressed up for that Mr. Maldon he may wake up to his responsibilities!'

Amy called to her maid as she went into her room, but the faithful Molly was already there with rose-water in a bowl and a scented towel. Together they worked on her appearance, the maid enjoying it perhaps more than the mistress. Amy was preoccupied; it was strange how her little interview with Mr. Maldon had affected her.

As she came downstairs later she heard her father's voice raised in anger. She paused on the staircase, surprised. Although he sometimes lost his temper, he had good manners that ought to have prevented an outbreak while guests were present. A moment's eavesdropping told her he was speaking to one of the menservants.

'And where,' he roared, 'did you find eighteen shillings for a shawl, sir?'

She heard a mumbled reply as she hurried downstairs to join him and perhaps soothe him back into good humour.

'Out of your wages?' cried Mr. Tyrell. 'You've saved eighteen shillings out of

26

half a year's wages? Let me tell you, sir, that you're a financial genius! Sir Robert Walpole could not have done so much!'

She had reached the cool dimness of the hall now, to find her father confronting Stephen Boles, one of the footmen, a man for whom she had no affection. All the same, she mustn't allow Papa to berate him a few yards away from the drawing-room door where their friends could hear.

Even as she thought this, Mr. Maldon came into the hall from the drawing-room. 'Is anything wrong, sir?' he inquired, leaning a little forward from his great height to see into the darkness of the hall after the brightness of the company room.

'Nay, sir, what do you think of this rogue? All at once he buys a costly shawl for his sweetheart Nancy, and tells me he saved the money when we both know he earns insufficient to have done it.'

Maldon met Amy's eyes across her father's shoulder. He understood the message flashed to him. 'Well, Mr. Tyrell, we both know that servants can have little extra occupations that bring in a trifle—'

'Aye, and I know what this rascal has done. Tell me the truth, Stephen Boles— you dealt with the smugglers last week when you were sent into Poole for provisions, did you not? Bought cheaply from them, and kept the difference in price to yourself?'

'No, sir, I swear, sir,' Stephen Boles began. 'I never went near the smugglers, sir. I met a man at an inn—'

'Don't lie to me, sir! A man at an inn! So he stopped you and offered you Bohea tea at one-third the correct price, and you expect me to believe you didn't know he was a smuggler? And in any case, what have you to say for the dishonesty of pocketing the money?'

'Papa dearest,' Amy interposed, coming to him with a rustle of taffeta and taking his arm, 'pray don't be so angry with him. He did it to buy Nancy a shawl for her birthday—did you not, Stephen?'

'Little enough to buy her,' Boles growled, 'since she gets such poor pay and has nothing to spend on herself—'

'Nancy gets paid the same as any other kitchen-maid,' Mr. Tyrell interrupted.

28

'Are you taking it upon you to stir up discontent among my household staff, sirrah?'

'Mr. Tyrell, I think he only meant—'

'Perhaps so, perhaps so, Mr. Maldon. But you won't defend a man who hob-nobs with smugglers?'

'But you have not quite established that he did that, sir.'

'He bought tea from a man who offered it to him at a discount price. It has to be either stolen or smuggled—that's common sense, sir. And that being so, Mr. Maldon, I think you'll agree I have a right to be indignant.'

'Well, it's certainly true that—'

'So you'll have to go, Boles. I won't have you in my house. I abhor dishonesty, and even more the activities of the smugglers, who undermine our entire society! As a justice of the peace it's my duty to stamp on smuggling and all who support it—and so there's an end to it, Boles! You'll leave my house this night.'

'Oh, Mr. Tyrell, sir, pray don't turn me away, sir.'

'What else do you expect? I won't have a thief and a supporter of contrabandists—'

'But without a character, Mr. Tyrell, I'll never get another place.'

'You should have thought of that before! You'll be out of this house before sunset, sir, or I'll take a whip to you.'

Boles, small and broad-shouldered, abandoned his pretence of contrition. He shot a venomous glance at his master and turned away. 'So much the worse for you!' he snarled over his shoulder as he stamped off.

'What did you say? Come back here this instant!'

But the footman had disappeared through the door to the servants' quarters.

Mr. Tyrell turned a wrathful glance on his daughter. 'And that's the man you were trying to intercede for,' he muttered.

'Yes, Papa, I believe I was wrong in thinking he meant no harm,' she agreed. 'But you are very naughty to lose your temper like that. Didn't you promise me you would never do it again after you frightened poor Mr. Hoddilow over those pigs he tried to sell you?'

Despite himself, Mr. Tyrell laughed.

'Confounded rogue,' he explained to Mr. Maldon. 'Tried to sell me pigs weighing two hundredweight after he'd poured water into them to make them heavy! I tell you, Mr. Maldon, there are few honest men in this world!'

He pushed his grey wig straight and allowed himself to be shepherded back into the drawing-room where his wife was flirting mildly with Beau Gramont. 'Look here, Eliza,' he addressed her, 'what were you thinking of to allow smuggled tea into our kitchens?'

Mrs. Tyrell, startled, snapped her fan shut and turned to stare at him. 'Smuggled tea, my dear?'

'Didn't you see that there was no Customs tag on the bag? Really, Eliza—' his voice rose a little—'it's sheer carelessness. What would people say if they knew? I, who am so hot on the trail of the smugglers—'

'Ah, George,' Beau Gramont said with a flashing grin that showed his fine teeth. 'It's a hard role you've chosen! A magistrate who sets his face against the Pegmen has to watch his step.'

'Pooh,' said Mr. Tyrell, throwing himself into a tapestry chair, 'it's little enough to do, when one considers the risks taken by the riding officers. Poor Rivers ...!'

Rivers was a Customs officer with a stretch of coastline under his jurisdiction which, like others, he had to watch by riding its length several times a week. During the previous month he had been found dead on the beach, stretched out to drown by the tide after the fashion of the smugglers who terrorised the district—pegged down by his wrists and ankles to await the incoming waves. It was from this style of getting even with their enemies that they were known as the Pegmen.

'If anyone asks my opinion,' said Gramont, 'Rivers was a fool. We all know that dozens of the riding officers are in the pay of the Pegmen—why could he not have been less honourable?'

'Come, Beau, that's no way to talk,' Mr. Tyrell protested. 'They are very brave men, risking their lives and sometimes losing them.'

'The more fools they!'

'I can't help thinking,' Bernard put in, 'that it's excessively foolish to ride around

the countryside in an exciseman's uni-
form. One could say it's truly asking for
trouble!'

'Which they get,' Maldon countered.

'Oh, so you defend them, do you? I
think it foolish, and useless too,' Bernard
said.

Amy saw her father bridle at Bernard's
words, and interposed hastily to prevent
an argument. Of course it was all a joke,
but her father took it so seriously. He held
that the Pegmen harmed the countryside
in a hundred different ways—not only did
they break the laws enacted by Parliament, but they took horses and cattle to
transport their smuggled goods, made
farmers hide the tea and tobacco in their
outhouses, and lorded it over the local in-
habitants like robber barons.

Others might say that the taxes on
goods such as tea, spirits, lace and tobacco were iniquitous, and that smugglers
were doing their friends a favour by land-
ing such cargoes on lonely beaches at
night. Amy's father believed that if the
law was wrong it should be changed in
Parliament, not flouted by ruthless men
for their own gain. Amy was inclined to

think he was right. But she didn't want an argument about it now.

So she soothed him now with gentle protests, and charmed Bernard away from his conversation with inquiries about the horse he intended to buy.

Mr. Maldon was so depressed by the sight that he took his leave as soon as he could, immediately the meal was over and without waiting to share the port with the gentlemen after the ladies had left them. Amy heard him go out to the stables to get his horse, and for some reason drifted to the window of the drawing-room in time to see him ride down the drive. If he had glanced back, she might have waved a farewell.

But he did not.

When at length the men came to the drawing-room for tea, it immediately appeared that something had happened to mar the tranquillity of the evening. To Amy's experienced eye it was clear that her father was vexed; he was silent and grim, and she saw his glance turn, with something like bewilderment, towards the Gramonts, father and son. It was some jibe against the Government, no doubt, of which he was an ardent supporter. She sighed inwardly. How cross gentlemen became over politics!

She asked Bernard what had occurred. He shrugged. 'Your father wants troops out,' he said. 'How the farmers would love that! Cavalry riding down the corn ...' He went on for some moments in rather ironic comment on Mr. Tyrell's proposals, so that she had no chance to lead him on to more romantic topics.

One way and another, she reflected wearily while Molly undressed her, it had been a most unsatisfactory day. First Mr. Maldon and the perplexity of how to treat him; her father in a rage with Stephen Boles, and in a pet with his friends; and finally her disappointment with Bernard. Why it should seem so important that Bernard should have declared himself today, she couldn't tell. But she felt as if some last, precious opportunity were slipping out of her hands.

Perhaps it was the weather that caused this mood of depression. The wind had dropped during dinner; now a strange heavy calm prevailed. A good storm would clear the air, she felt. At length, oppressed by the heaviness of the air under the tester, she got out of bed and leaned out of the window.

Outside everything was still. The garden was like a painted scene, all silver and shadow—the garden of an enchanter.

Then she heard the creak of the postern gate that gave access between the Tyrell's grounds and Parall. A figure crossed the lawn and made its way rapidly towards the door of the garden room. She recognised that tall, portly figure—recognised the mood implied by that rapid, plunging walk. It was her father, and in a temper.

She drew back and stood listening for him to climb the stairs, but the footsteps didn't come. Presumably he had gone to pace himself into calmness, up and down the library, as he often did.

She sighed and lay down in her bed again. Being awake and aware did her no good; she had better try what sleep could do.

The next thing she was conscious of was a tremendous hammering which seemed at first to be inside her head. But when she sat up in alarm she found that the noise came from downstairs. It was a tattoo upon the oaken front door.

A moment later it ceased abruptly as the butler went to answer it. A moment's silence, then in the morning sunlight she heard Palmer hurrying up the stairs.

'Mr. Tyrell! Mr. Tyrell!' he cried, knocking and calling at the door of her parents' room. 'Oh, Mr. Tyrell, please come at once. Mr. Gramont is dead!'

CHAPTER 2

At first Amy's heart had turned to stone. She thought the butler meant Bernard. But by the time she had found her dressing-gown and gone out, the true facts were being revealed.

Beau Gramont had been found dead in the hall of Parall, killed by a blow from a dagger.

Mr. Tyrell must go at once, as the local magistrate, to see that an inquiry was started. The village constable was scarcely capable of dealing with this. 'May I come too, Papa?' Amy asked. 'Mrs Gramont may need help.'

'She has daughters, Amy—'

'But sir, they will be overcome! You know how they all adored their father.'

He hesitated. 'Very well,' he said. 'But be quick.'

She dressed with trembling haste and was with him as he hurried out of the

38

house. It took only a few moments to reach the entrance hall of Parall, but at the front door the constable, John Day, put himself in her way. ' 'Tisn't suitable for a lady, Miss Tyrell,' he mumbled. 'Be so good as to go through the side door.'

She did as she was bid without demur and hurried upstairs to Mrs. Gramont's bedroom. There she found her with her three daughters, and which of them was most in need of her support it was difficult to say. Mrs. Gramont herself was prostrate with grief, incapable of forming a sentence. Janet, white as marble, was trying to make her take some soothing tincture. The two younger girls were huddled together in a duet of tears.

Time flew by as Amy helped get Mrs. Gramont to sleep and persuaded Janet to go to her room and dress. The others, Mildred and Patty, she coaxed into coming downstairs to take control of the servants, who were wandering about without direction. By dint of hard work she got a meal cooked that served as an early dinner, though Janet refused to eat and Mrs. Gramont remained in the thrall of her semi-unconsciousness.

About two o'clock in the afternoon her father came in search of her. 'Come, Amy, we must go,' he said.

'Go?'

'Fetch your shawl—ah, you have it. Then come along.'

'But, Papa—I am needed—'

'Someone else will have to take charge. We cannot stay.'

'Cannot? I don't understand you, Papa.'

Her father flushed. 'The fact is, Amy ...'

'What?'

He cleared his throat. 'They've asked me to go.'

'Asked you to—? Who has asked you?'

'The constable—and Bernard.'

'Bernard doesn't want you here. But, in Heaven's name, Papa, why not?'

'Because, Amy ...' He paused and sought for words. 'Because a magistrate ought not to conduct a case in which he must give evidence.'

'Evidence?' She caught at his arm. 'I don't understand. What evidence can you possibly give?'

'We need not discuss that. In the meantime I must not stay here, child. So come along.'

'But Papa, even if you go, surely I ought to stay?'

Mr. Tyrell put a heavy arm around her shoulders. 'My dear, you force me to say it. Bernard wishes us both out of this house.'

His words were like a wave of cold water dashing over her. She gasped. Then, white-lipped, she went without further protest.

As they were going out of the door Constable Day came hurrying up, his plump face creased in dismay at what he was about to say.

'Excuse me, sir—before you go—you'll promise not to leave the district before the inquest?'

Mr. Tyrell drew himself up. 'Certainly I'll not leave the district! Why should I?' He turned and strode away, leaving Amy to run after him with her hands to her burning cheeks at the insult.

When they reached home, Amy's mother was sitting expectantly in the drawing-room. 'Well, how did it happen? I always said one day Beau Gramont would meet a jealous husband who wouldn't be satisfied with easy explanations. A duel, was it?'

'No, my dear, the man was stabbed in the back.'

'George!' Mrs. Tyrell's eyes went wide. 'You mean he was *murdered*?' After a moment she added, 'The Pegmen, I suppose.'

'That may be,' her husband said. 'Let us not discuss it, Mrs. Tyrell. I should be glad of some coffee and food.'

'Of course, my dear, of course! Ring the bell, Amy. What an *extraordinary* occurrence. One isn't safe in one's home! Do you recall that earlier this year they set upon a poor landowner in Hampshire who wouldn't allow them to store their goods in his stable? They threw him down a well, poor soul. Well, well, God protect us, I say.' She went out to supervise the making of the snack.

The next twenty-four hours were dismal and full of suspense. Mr. Tyrell retired to his library, refusing to be with his family except at mealtimes. Mrs. Tyrell complained bitterly to Amy about it. 'Most inconsiderate! At such a time, when a neighbour has met his end! Surely he can see I need his comfort and re-assurance?'

'I pray, Mama, don't insist on his company for the moment. He is very upset.'

'And so am I! You know, Beau Gramont and I were the greatest of friends! He used to say such things to me—!But I always told him that my heart belonged to Mr. Tyrell, of course.'

'Oh, Mama, Beau Gramont flirted with everyone! It meant nothing.'

'So you say, my love,' Mrs. Tyrell said, a little put out, 'but you are too young to understand that a man can flirt with all and have special feelings for one.'

Seeing that her mother was determined to build up a legend that Beau Gramont had been secretly in love with her, Amy dropped the subject.

The inquest was held on the Thursday at the Garland Inn in Markledon. The coroner was Mr. Pierce, her father's lawyer and a friend, a visitor, too, that fatal evening.

Evidence was given by the housemaid of finding the body when she came downstairs to light the kitchen fire. The surgeon stated the cause of death, a blow from a dagger which formed part of a display of Italian weapons on the wainscot of the hall.

Next came Bernard, whom Amy had not once set eyes on since the evening before his father's death.

Yes, he had been the last member of the household to see Mr. Gramont alive. They had had a glass of wine together after returning from Mr. Tyrell's house. Then he, Bernard, had gone to bed.

'Did you hear or see anything unusual?'

'No, Mr. Pierce.'

The next witness, to Amy's surprise, was Stephen Boles.

'Now,' said Mr. Pierce rather severely when the oath had been administered, 'I understand you came forward with some information of your own accord. Please tell the court what you told the constable.'

'Yes, sir,' said Boles, wiping sweat from his chin with his neckcloth. 'Well, I was at Parall, Mr. Gramont's house, on that night.'

'Why were you there?'

'Well, sir, you must know Mr. Tyrell

had turned me out in one of his fits of temper, and I'd nowhere to go.'

There was a rustle from the public assembled in the large taproom of the Garland.

'Keep to the point, Stephen Boles,' said Mr. Pierce, straightening his fusty old wig. 'I asked you why you were at Parall?'

'Well, me and Canoway, Mr. Gramont's butler, are acquainted. I thought he'd probably let me have a bed for the night. Which he did.'

'And?'

'We sat up, your worship, pretty late, playing cards. And about half past twelve I went out to cross to the stables—Canoway had had a pallet put there for me.'

'Well, go on.'

'As I passed Mr. Gramont's study, I saw a light in the window, so I looked in, 'cos the shutters weren't closed on account of the hot weather. And I saw Mr. Tyrell there with him.'

'Mr. Tyrell? At midnight?'

'I saw him, sir.'

'Yes? Well?'

'They was having a row, sir. Going at

it hammer and tongs. At least, Mr. Tyrel
was. Mr. Gramont, he was leaning back
laughing.'

Through Amy's mind passed the picture of her father walking angrily across
the moonlit garden. What Stephen Boles
was saying was true. Her father had been
at Parall that night.

'Did you hear what was said?' Mr.
Pierce asked Boles.

'Oh no, sir. I should have had to go
right up to the casement and listen, and
I couldn't do that, sir,' Boles said
virtuously.

'Quite right, quite right,' Mr. Pierce
agreed, blowing out a breath. His little
red face was growing more and more perturbed. 'Did you go to bed then?'

'Well, I went back to the kitchen to tell
Canoway what I'd seen, sir. He'll tell you
I did, if you ask him. And *then* I went
to bed.'

Canoway was called and agreed that
Boles had stayed overnight at Parall—
had, moreover, come back to the butler's
pantry after starting off for the stables,
to report that a quarrel was going on between Squire Tyrell and Mr. Gramont.

'But you yourself didn't see it?'

'No, sir, not my business.'

George Tyrell then took the stand.

'Now, Mr. Tyrell,' said the lawyer with reluctance, 'this is—I'm sure you understand—very difficult. Please tell us, in your own words, what happened at this interview with Mr. Gramont.'

'There was no interview,' Mr. Tyrell said coolly.

'Have you nothing to say in answer to the allegation that you and Mr. Gramont had a quarrel?'

'Nothing.'

'But Mr. Tyrell, Stephen Boles saw you.'

'The man has a grudge against me because I dismissed him.'

'But, come now, George,' begged Mr. Pierce, 'be reasonable! Canoway also says—'

'Canoway says he saw no quarrel. He only heard of it from Boles. And Boles is not to be trusted. You would not take his word against mine, Edward?'

Mr. Pierce fidgeted under the gaze of his old friend but could think of nothing further to say that would help. He sent the coroner's jury away to consider their verdict; they trooped out into the Garland's cellar and then came back fifteen minutes later.

'Well, gentlemen of the jury, have you reached a verdict?'

'We have, Mr. Pierce, sir.'

The foreman looked at the others. They nodded. 'We find that Mr. Gramont was murdered ...'

'Murdered,' quoted Mr. Pierce, writing.

'... By Mr. Tyrell.'

Mr. Pierce's quill was arrested as it began to trace the "M" of Mr.

'What's that you say, Tim Benworth?'

Benworth rubbed the back of his neck with the palm of his hand. 'Why, sir,' he said, 'we're of the opinion that it's plain as the nose on your face that Mr. Tyrell did it in one of his rages. So we say he should be taken into custody for trial before the Assizes. And that's our verdict.'

'No,' gasped Amy, starting to her feet.

'Quiet, Miss Tyrell,' admonished Constable Day.

Mr. Pierce argued and objected, but

the jury were adamant. Staring at them, Amy saw that they were not the friendly villagers she had always thought them but—today—men of power who were enjoying the idea of bringing her father low. Many of them had had the rough side of Mr. Tyrell's tongue; he had made enemies, it appeared.

'Very well,' Mr. Pierce said at last, pursing and unpursing his lips so that his plump cheeks quivered. 'I must accept it, I suppose.'

At these words, Amy felt herself go faint with incredulous horror. Around her people were making sounds of approval; some even went so far as to applaud. Her mother seized her arm. 'Daughter, what does it mean?' she cried.

'Hush, Mama—'

'But they cannot arrest your father?'

The constable, John Day, made his way across the taproom until he came face to face with Mr. Tyrell. 'Sir, I must ask you to accompany me—'

'No!' cried Amy. 'It's all a stupid mistake!'

Day looked round uneasily. 'I know, miss,' he said. 'But what else can I do?

Mr. Tyrell, I'm sure you won't make no trouble, sir.'

Amy's father stood up and pulled straight the fronts of his waistcoat. 'I shall make no trouble, John. But I should like some dinner before I go to gaol—and I should like a word with my wife, if you've no objection.'

'None at all, sir,' said Day, shuffling his feet.

Mrs. Tyrell was clinging to Amy's arm. Gently Amy detached herself. 'I will go outside and wait, Papa,' she said in a voice she kept tolerably steady. 'Pray send for me when you have spoken with my mother.'

She walked away, anxious to be out of sight before the tears spilled over on to her cheeks. She reached the door of the room, then paused, wondering where to go. People were milling around her; some jostled her without apology, others drew away from her. She reached the door of the inn and saw Lady Frier's carriage waiting some way up the main street. Ah, she thought, I'll ask her ladyship to let me sit in the carriage for a few minutes.

She walked up the uneven pavement.

The coachman was on the box as if ready to start, so she hastened her step. 'Pray, your ladyship—' she began, looking in at the carriage window.

'Excuse me, Miss Tyrell,' interrupted the lady. 'I'm in rather a hurry. Drive on, Jack!'

The coachman flicked his whip, the two horses strained forward, the carriage rolled away. Lady Frier didn't even trouble herself to lean forward and wave a farewell.

It was so like an actual slap on the face that Amy felt her cheeks burn. She swung on her heel and hurried down the nearest alley, heedless of where she was going, almost running in her need to expunge the insult by physical activity.

When she got back to the Garland there was a crowd still waiting by the entrance. They parted to allow her to go through. In the small saloon to the left of the hall she found her father sitting before a table on which, untasted, lay bread, cold meat, and Madeira. Her mother was sitting by his side, her handkerchief over her face.

'Dearest child,' Mr. Tyrell said, rising, 'this will be a bad time for all of us, but most of all for your mother. She is unaccustomed to the difficulties of everyday life. Promise me you will care for her, shield her?'

'I promise, Papa.'

'You are my jewel,' he said with deepest affection, taking her hand in both of his. 'Forgive me, Amy ...'

'For what, sir?' she asked, astounded.

'For wrecking your chance of happiness with Bernard.'

'Papa!' For a moment she thought he meant that he *had* in actual fact killed Bernard's father. Then better sense took over. 'You mean by somehow becoming involved in this foolish muddle? It isn't your fault, sir. And I warrant you it will soon all be cleared up.'

The constable, who had stood silent inside the door, moved warningly. 'The coach is ready to take you to Winchester, sir,' he muttered. 'I can see it coming up the street.'

'No, no!' wept Mrs. Tyrell. 'No, a moment more, constable—'

'I daresn't, ma'am. There's those that want your husband safe away from here before the crowd takes the law into its own hands. Beau Gramont had many friends in this town.'

'You are right,' Amy's father said with quick acceptance. 'And the sooner our farewells are over, the better. Come, Eliza, be brave. Dry your tears. You're making your eyes red—you don't want to go out in public looking a fright, do you?'

'I don't care!' sobbed Mrs. Tyrell. Her lack of care of her appearance was the measure of her grief. 'George, George, your temper was always your worst fault!'

'Mama,' Amy interposed, 'that is no way to talk.'

'She's overset,' Mr. Tyrell said. 'She doesn't mean it.' He patted his wife on the shoulder. 'Do you, my love?'

'Yes, I do, for this is no moment to pretend,' cried his wife. 'You've always been jealous of Beau Gramont, George! But surely it need not have led to *this?*'

Horror-stricken, Amy took her mother from her father's grasp and held her close while the constable escorted him from the room. She heard the growling of the crowd as he was taken out, heard the door of the closed coach being slammed shut, heard the horses' hooves clatter on the cobbles and the grinding as the wheels turned.

She thrust her mother down upon a chair and ran out. The coach was drawing away. 'Papa, Papa!' she called.

He couldn't look out. The windows were fastened and the blinds drawn down.

'Papa, I'll attend to everything! Don't be afraid, Papa! In a few days it will all be cleared up! Papa! Papa!'

And she stood in the middle of the road, a small figure in mist-grey silk gown and lace cap, watching the carriage recede as it took her father to prison.

CHAPTER 3

One of the hardest things for Amy to bear in the days that followed was her mother's complete acceptance of her father's guilt. She argued, pleaded and stormed. Her mother nodded but remained unconvinced. To all Amy's protests that her father was incapable of harming an old friend she would answer, 'You know his temper, daughter.'

And since Amy was working against the memory of that glimpse in the moonlight of that angry figure, she was soon arguing for the sake of convincing herself.

She and her mother were ostracised; former friends paid no visits, shared newspapers were not sent on, small services were discontinued. Messages of inquiry were sent by Amy to Parall, concerning the health of Mrs. Gramont, were ignored. Bernard did not come, did not even trouble to walk a few yards out of his way so that they could have a moment's conversation or explanation.

One by one the servants at the Manor House disappeared from the scene. The coachman, the grooms, cook and the kitchen-maids, Mrs. Tyrell's personal maid ... The faithful few remained: Palmer the butler, Bryce the under-gardener, Amy's own maid Molly. It was a strange household—quiet, subdued, with an air of suspended animation. Without the forceful and emphatic Squire, the place had lost its life-force.

The greatest problem of all was finding legal advice. Amy naturally turned to Mr. Pierce, a lifelong friend of her father's, but received a hard blow.

'Why now, y'see, m'dear,' he said, pulling at the sides of his dusty wig, 'I can't act for you. In view of the fact that I was the coroner who committed your father for trial.'

'But you are his lawyer, Uncle Pierce!' she protested.

'Of course, of course. Had I known how the inquest was going to turn out, I should have refused to act as coroner— and then, d'ye see, I'd be free now to take on his defence. But I can't.'

'Of course you can!'

'Nay, child, I *cannot*. It's against the rules of procedure. Your father will have to look elsewhere for his defence lawyer.'

She sat silent, eyes downcast, trying to come to terms with this shattering disappointment. After a long moment she drew a breath and said, 'Then whom do you recommend, sir?'

Mr. Pierce fidgeted with the inkstand on his desk. 'Well, now, Amy, there you have me! I'm at a loss what to say.'

'Why so?'

'Because ... well, because, child, I don't believe you'll find a man in the whole of Hampshire who'll take on the case.'

'What?' She stared at him. 'You can't be serious, sir!'

'Never more so, child. Your father is neatly caught in a trap from which there seems to be no escape. You must have guessed, my dear, that every man on that coroner's jury was either a smuggler or a supporter of the smuggler's trade?'

'You mean that—?'

'It was what we call 'a packed jury'— they had seen their chance to rid themselves of a magistrate who was a thorn in their side, and they took it. Stephen Boles, the chief accuser, he's one of their minions, I'd take my oath. And Tim Benworth, that acted as foreman of the jury—the riding officer of the Customs Department has told me more than once that he suspected Benworth of being a chief participant. David Bartholomew, the riding officer—a shrewd fellow, that. He said he was on the watch for evidence to charge Benworth, but so far had never got it.'

'But why did you allow Benworth to act as foreman?' Amy cried. 'Why did you let such men take part?'

'How could I prevent it, my dear? Three-quarters of the population is either in league with the Pegmen or in fear of them. It's impossible to pick a jury without including supporters of the Pegmen. And besides, how could I know Boles was going to produce a tale like that? I'm not in the confidence of such people, Amy, and once they had given the verdict I had to accept it.'

Amy felt as if she were stifling. 'I can't believe it, sir,' she cried. 'Are you saying that my father is as good as dead, for want of a lawyer—'

'I'm saying, my love, that any man who takes on the case may find himself in like straits—and we all know it.'

'But what becomes of justice then?'

'Aye, what indeed?' the old man sighed.

'Have you no advice for me, Uncle Pierce? No help in my attempts to save my father?'

He huddled into himself. 'Don't be angry, Amy. I'm like everyone else. I'm afraid too. I don't want to end up stretched out in the sands waiting for the tide to kill me. I want to die in my bed.'

Useless to talk it over with her mother; Mrs. Tyrell had so completely convinced herself that her husband had killed Beau Gramont in a fit of jealous anger that her only thought was to beg him to throw himself on the mercy of the court. There was no one else to whom she could turn except her father himself. She decided to set out for Winchester next day.

Her mother was aghast at the plan. 'Go to Winchester?' she quavered. 'To the ... to the prison?'

'Since that is where my father is, Mama, yes, I must go to the prison.'

'But ... but it's so unpleasant there, I hear! And unhealthy!'

'Aye, ma'am,' Amy said in a hard tone, 'and my father is locked up there!'

The journey was uneventful if one discounted the bad roads and Bryce's bad driving. The poor man had never handled a coach and four, but since there was no coachman he undertook the task. They went off the road several times and nearly overturned once, but at length they came into the town of Winchester as the light was fading. Amy was tense and full of apprehension at the interview that lay ahead; she intended to ask her father, pointblank, if he had harmed Beau Gramont.

And she was not quite certain of the reply she would receive.

Jeffrey Maldon got his first news of the case in his copy of the *London Daily Gazetteer.* He was sitting in a coffee-house off the Strand, passing away a morning while he awaited a summons to the office of Mr. Pitt. When, on turning the page of his newspaper, he came across the name of Mr. Tyrell, he gave an exclamation that caused his neighbour to spill his morning chocolate.

'Why, what ails you, sir?' the man complained.

'Your pardon, sir. I have just seen something that surprised me mightily.' He read the column with growing dismay: Mr. Tyrell arrested on evidence of an eye-witness to a quarrel, Beau Gramont dead ... 'Good God!' he burst out, and got to his feet so roughly that he rocked the table and caused his neighbour to spill the remains of the chocolate.

'Damme, sir, take care!'

'Forgive me, and let me pass, sir. I'm in a hurry.'

'To do what, i'faith?'

'To get back to Markledon.'

'But Mr. Maldon!' was the reply. 'You have an appointment with Mr. Pitt!'

'Mr. Pitt will survive the disappointment.'

'Sir,' said Mr. Pitt's chief secretary, 'the Paymaster-General does not like to be treated with disrespect.'

'Then devil take the Paymaster-General!' cried Jeffrey Maldon as he hurried out.

He fetched his horse from the livery stables and was on his way within the hour. The route led via Guildford and Winchester to Ringwood and the Hampshire coast, a busy and dusty road but hard underfoot, so that at least he was not delayed by bogged-down wagons or impassable quagmires. The thirty-mile climb to Farnham over the Hog's Back tired his mount; he led him for the next hour saying soothingly, 'There now, Gylo, good old fellow, take your rest, for we must push on again as soon as you're ready.'

There were still forty miles to go to Winchester. It was already well past noon. Yet in this fine autumn weather the light would hold a long while yet, and if he didn't press Gylo too hard they could reach the cathedral city without killing themselves and in time to find a bed for the night.

Gylo, as if he knew what was expected of him, tossed his head and snorted when the road opened out ahead of him on the downward side of the hill. Maldon allowed him a drink at the next brook, while he himself washed his dust-streaked face, and then off they went at an easy canter that ate up the miles.

Winchester was a city that Maldon knew quite well. Although it was late evening as he trotted Gylo past the Butter Cross, the shops were still open and the tradesmen were out catching at passers-by, begging them to buy. There ahead, he could see a hubbub—a coach stalled in the crossroad, horses trampling and shying at the catcalls of a crowd who surged about them.

'Tyrell, Tyrell, we'll hang him like a squirrel!' they chanted. 'Pegmen for ever, Excisemen never!'

Maldon drew rein. What on earth were they about? What sense did it make, to beset a passenger in a coach, calling out against George Tyrell? Tyrell was in prison, safe from their abuse.

Unless ...

He dug his heels into Gylo's sides and went ahead at a fast trot. The men nearest him scattered a little at his approach, not in fear but simply so as not to be kicked by the big black's hooves. They expected him to go past. He did not, he stopped alongside the coach. One glance showed him the Tyrells' initials on the panel. Regardless of whom he hit, he rode Gylo sideways, using his whip on the by-standers to clear a way.

Inside the carriage a small figure was huddled into a corner. He leaned forward and tapped on the glass with his crop. 'Miss Tyrell?'

He saw her brush clenced fists up against her cheeks. She was very frightened—and with reason.

'Take heart, Miss Tyrell. It's Jeffrey Maldon.'

'Mr. Maldon!' Her voice came to him faintly through the carriage door. 'Oh, Mr. Maldon!'

She slid down the glass a little. Her face was pale as she leaned towards it. 'Sir, can you tell me what has happened to Bryce?'

'Bryce?'

'He was driving the carriage.'

There was no one in the box. 'He's gone, I'm afraid, ma'am. Run off in the face of—'

'No, indeed, sir,' she interrupted, her voice rising in reproof. 'They dragged him off his seat. Oh, poor Bryce, poor dear man, I hope they haven't hurt him.'

'Where were you going, Miss Tyrell?'

'I scarcely know, sir. To find an inn before setting out to see my father.'

'Very well,' he said. 'Let's see what can be done.'

He forced Gylo through the few men who stood between him and the driving seat of the carriage. He swung up to it from Gylo's back. The reins had fallen between the two near horses, but his long arm reached down to retrieve them. 'Up, then, my beauties,' he said, snapping the leather against their backs. 'Up, *walk* on, *walk* on!'

A howl of anger arose as the crowd understood his intentions. 'Tyrell's man, Tyrell's man!' they shouted, clutching at the side of the coach.

But the horses, frightened by the hub-bub, were only too eager to move. They plunged forward, scattering those ahead of the coach. One or two rascals began to walk alongside, banging on the sides of the vehicle to frighten Amy, but at a whistle from Maldon Gylo began to canter from one side to the other, crowding the walkers against the wheels so that good sense told them to retire. By the time they turned into Jewry and drew up beside the George Inn, the escort had fallen away.

The ostlers came forward to unhitch the horses. Maldon jumped down from the box and opened the carriage door. Without waiting to put down the step, and scarcely thinking what he was about, he swung her down in his arms. She clung to him in relief and gratitude.

'Miss Tyrell!' he said. 'Are you all right?'

'Faith, sir, if you discount a bad attack of the trembles, I'm well enough,' she said in a voice that shook.

'But what are you doing here, ma'am. And with no footman nor maid?'

'I ... It's a long story, sir. I'll bore you with it later, if you'll permit. But I'll say this, Mr. Maldon—I was never so glad to see anyone in my life!'

He stood gazing down at her, one arm still around her to support her, and for a moment she saw a blaze in those grey eyes that took her aback. But in a moment it was gone, and he was all urbane politeness. 'Let me take you indoors,' he said, 'and bespeak a room. Then when we have sent for some refreshments perhaps you will make me *au fait* with what has been happening.'

The keeper of the famous George Inn was justly proud of his accommodations. A comfortable room was put at Amy's disposal, her portmanteau was brought up, she washed the grime of travel from her face and set in order the tight curls of her lightly powdered hair. Then, much restored, she went down to the private parlour where the tea things had been set.

Mr. Maldon was already there. He said at once, 'To set your mind at rest, I have made inquiries for Bryce and I hear he took refuge in a haberdasher's shop. I have sent to fetch him here to you.'

'Thank you, Mr. Maldon. I couldn't forgive myself if harm had come to him.'

'And you? What has been happening to you? I read the news in the London paper.'

'Aye, sir. A strange affair, isn't it? A justice of the peace arrested by his own parishioners.' Quickly, without undue emphasis on the pain her family had endured, she told him what had occurred

and why she was here in Winchester: to
see her father and receive his instructions

'Come, sit down,' Maldon said, leading
her to an elbow-chair. 'You have had a
bad experience here, but there's no reason
to believe the animosity towards your
father will last long. Once you have found
a lawyer to take the case, everything will
become easier. I should like to think I
could be useful to you, Miss Tyrell. If you
will tell me to whom I should apply to
offer my service, I will do so as soon as
I can.'

'Thank you, sir. You are very kind. But
... but there is no one to whom I can send
you.'

'I don't follow you. Who is standing
in place of your father—who is in the role
of head of the family? Mr. Pierce?'

'No, Mr. Maldon. He is, alas, he is too
frightened to play any part.'

'Then ... Bernard?'

She flushed. 'Bernard has not spoken
or written to me since the death of his
father. All my messages to his mother
have been ignored.' She paused to clear
her throat. 'It is in times like this that we
learn who are our friends.'

Mr. Maldon, who had been leaning over her, straightened and stared over her bent head. 'Do I take it, then, that you are utterly alone in this distress?'

'Save for my mother and some of the servants who, God bless them, have refused to be frightened away. That is why I was travelling unattended—my maid is at home with my mother. She is not fit to be left alone without the support of a female companion. We are shunned both by those who believe my father guilty and those who do not. The latter dare not help us—they have had threats from the Pegmen.'

Jeffrey Maldon went to the tea-tray and poured the hot brew into the thick china of the George Inn. He brought the cup to her.

'I'm glad I came,' he said. 'I was in two minds to turn back again at Farnham—it seemed too ridiculous to suppose you'd need me.'

'You've come all the way from London on our account?'

He nodded.

'But you had business in London, had you not?'

'Oh, that ...' A dismissive wave settled the matter of the Paymaster-General and would-be Prime Minister of England. 'That can be attended to another time.'

'I simply cannot express how grateful—'

'Please.' He stopped her with a little shake of his head, and she smiled and sighed.

'The best proof of gratitude would be a plate of cold beef,' she said, aiming at lightness, 'for I imagine you did not stop to eat much on the way. Let's ring for the waiter and order some substantial refreshments.'

'Ma'am, if you would allow me, I should prefer to go to the prison to see your father.'

'What, now? At this late hour?'

'The turnkey will no doubt be willing to bestir himself for a shilling or so. There will be no difficulty.'

'I will come with you,' she said, setting aside her cup and preparing to rise.

'No, indeed!' He was shocked. 'Such a place is not fit for a lady at any time of day, and least of all at night.'

'If it is fit for my father, it is fit for me.'

He set her back in her chair with gentle hands. 'It is *not* fit for your father—he is there wrongfully and no doubt in great distress. Believe me, Miss Tyrell, as a lawyer it is often my task to visit those in custody and I have seen how stricken a man can be when his loved ones come to him there. Let me forewarn your father of your wish to visit him. Let him have a few hours to ready himself for it. It will be best, I assure you.'

She argued for a time, but in her heart she knew he was right. At length she said, 'Then if I must stay here I can at least make myself useful. I will see to it that a meal is waiting for you on your return.'

'Thank you. I imagine I shall be gone an hour or one hour and a half at most. Shall you wait up?'

She gave him a glance from her hazel eyes that spoke a thousand words.

'Very well, I shall see you then. *A bientôt.*'

While he was gone Amy gave the innkeeper of the George a great deal of trouble. She ordered a ragoût, then changed her mind on the grounds that the weather was too warm; cold beef would be better

71

after all. But then it was so plain ... Instead she would have cold duck prepared for Mr. Maldon, after the French style. But no, perhaps he had no taste for French sauces? She racked her brains, trying to recall what he had enjoyed at her father's table but, alas, on most occasions when he had dined at the Manor House Amy's attention had been on Bernard.

That done, she flew upstairs to the bedroom to up-end her portmanteau over the bed, seeking a change of clothes to make herself look less travel-worn. Too late now to regret that she had scolded Molly for spending too long on the packing. She had thought to be in Winchester overnight only, visiting her father and then hurrying back to Markledon with his advice and instructions about his defence. Because she knew he loved her in a particular dress, she had brought it with her—but it was a poor little thing, a cotton gown of sprigged pink and beige, harking back almost to her schoolgirl days.

Still, it was fresher to look upon than her travelling costume, so she put it on, struggling with the unaccustomed task of lacing herself and fastening the waist ties without a maid.

If she had paused to ask herself why it mattered so much to look attractive, she would have said it was because she owed it to a man who had come so far simply to be of use to her. She would have refused to listen to some faint inner voice that murmured she wished to please Mr. Maldon. Honest though she was as a rule, she could not allow herself to think that Jeffrey Maldon had made some inroads upon her feelings. She could still summon up a picture of his face, the day she told him he had no hope of gaining her affections, how sad he had looked then, how hurt and disappointed ...

Why had that memory stayed with her? It would have been more sensible to banish it for ever. Mr. Maldon's broken heart—if it *was* broken—should have been no concern of hers; and indeed she thought she had forgotten all about it. Yet as she surveyed herself in the glass she was hoping Mr. Maldon would find her pleasing, and that this new relationship between them would lead on to a lasting friendship. Yes, friendship ... Surely there could be friendship between a man and a woman? She nodded at her reflection

Her reflection nodded back, perhaps less certain than Amy that her feelings were perfectly under control.

When at last she went downstairs again, the cool late evening breeze was fluttering the curtains of the parlour. The time was nearly ten o'clock. She was a little apprehensive. Never in her life before had she been alone, away from home, awaiting the coming of a male companion at ten o'clock at night.

She heard his voice in the entrance lobby of the inn and flew to the door of the parlour. Her searching gaze tried to read something from his expression, but he was giving nothing away.

'How is he, sir?' she begged. 'How is my father?'

'Composed, ma'am, but not hopeful. I told him that you were here in Winchester, and he sends you his fondest love, but requests you not to go to the prison. He says—'

'Not go? Of course I shall go!'

'Miss Tyrell, if you truly love him you will not grieve him by insisting. He feels it a deep humiliation to be penned up like a criminal. He cannot bear to think of your seeing him in those conditions. In short, ma'am—I gave him my word I would prevent your visit.'

'You gave him your word—How dare you, sir! What right had you to take such a decision for me?' Amy's face was on fire with resentment and anger. 'You went there, you said, to prepare him for my visit tomorrow—'

'I went to find out what could be done for his defence,' he put in with calmness. 'In order to coax him to be frank with me, I must have his trust. I cannot gain it by going back on a promise to him.'

'But you had no right to promise.'

'I had the right of a lawyer acting in the interests of his client.'

'You take a great deal upon yourself, sir! *I* have not hired you!'

'You are not my client, Miss Tyrell. Your father is. *He* has hired me.'

'But this is most unfair! I thought you understood my feelings. If I had known how you were going to behave I should have—'

'What, Miss Tyrell? Hired another

lawyer?'

She gave a little gasp and checked the words that were springing to her lips. Of course there *was* no other lawyer. No one else but Mr Maldon would take the case. She could not afford to antagonise this arbitrary young man, because he was the only helper she had. She pressed her lips together and after struggling for composure said rather coldly. 'I have ordered a meal, Mr. Maldon. Are you ready to eat now?'

'Thank you. You are sharing it with me, I hope?'

She had somehow pictured herself sitting across from him in the candle-light in a spirit of complete accord. It hadn't occurred to her she would be bearing a grudge against him. As for the pink cotton dress, she no longer cared whether it was becoming to her or not. She went briskly to the bell-pull, summoned the waiter, and told him in a very peremptory tone to put the food on the table.

When she turned, it was to find Mr. Maldon watching her with ironic amusement. 'Faith, Miss Tyrell, you make your feelings known,' he remarked.

'But to little purpose, sir!'

'Listen, Amy. Your father's health is of the utmost importance at this time. He is in danger of sinking into a state of despairing inaction, a thing we must do all in our power to counteract.'

'Inaction?' she echoed. 'But my father has always been a most active and forth-right man.'

'That is my impression, too, from my short acquaintance with him. I was shock-ed at the change in him. We talked quite calmly and with complete understanding of each other, but I was conscious all the while that he does not really believe he can be saved from the rope.'

'Don't speak so!'

'Forgive me. I don't do it to distress you, only to show you how serious the matter is.' His calm eyes, of a strange clear grey like sea-ice, rested on her with compassion. 'He believes that the Pegmen are determined to see him hanged. He feels it is useless to explain himself in court because it will make no difference to the result. When I asked him to ac-count for the fact that Stephen Boles reported his presence at Parall that night, he merely shrugged.'

'He was there,' Amy said in a low voice, feeling something of her father's despair. 'I saw him come home at midnight. And he was angry. I fear Stephen Boles was speaking the truth.'

'On that very assumption, I pressed your father to account for the story. He no longer troubled to deny that he had been with Mr. Gramont, but repeated that it didn't matter, that he was as good as dead, like the murdered man. Then he said something very significant.'

'Pray, sir, what was that?' she queried, sitting forward in her seat.

'He said, "I must do what I can for the living, and that's best achieved by saying nothing. Once I'm out of the way, poor Amy can pick up her life again."'

She saw him watch her carefully as he reported the words. She let their meaning press in upon her and took her time before she spoke. 'He means that once he's dead, Bernard may one day forgive me for being the daughter of his father's murderer.'

'So I think too,' Maldon said. 'His first wish is for your happiness, since he feels he is doomed in any case.'

'You are very quick, sir,' she faltered. 'You understand my father's thoughts very well.'

'And is he correct?' he asked in a steady tone. 'Is he correct in thinking that your happiness depends on Bernard Gramont?'

It was days now since Amy had allowed her thoughts to dwell on Bernard. His absence, his silence, the way he had turned his back on her without even asking for her understanding—all these had hurt too much to dwell upon. Now, at Jeffrey Maldon's question, the grief welled up again. Her eyes brimmed with tears. She couldn't speak.

'I see it does,' Mr. Maldon said. 'Well, it is better to be aware of the stumbling-blocks ...'

The waiter came in at that moment with a great tray of silver dishes containing cold ham, turbot, veal pasty, and an apricot syllabub. During the few minutes that he spent clattering them out upon the table, Amy was able to recover herself.

'I hope it is what you like, sir,' she murmured, indicating the menu. 'I had to guess at your tastes.'

'It all looks delicious. And though I wasn't aware of it until I saw the food, I'm very hungry. Thank you.' He accepted the plate she offered him and paused. 'You will eat something too?'

'No, sir, I don't want anything.'

'Pray do, Miss Tyrell. I don't want you fainting from lack of food.'

'I'm not in the habit of fainting,' she said, rather crossly. 'Do you take me for a ninny?'

'Anything but, ma'am.'

She eyed him suspiciously, but he was busy putting glazed turbot on his plate. After he had swallowed a few mouthfuls he looked up, met her glance and said, 'Come, I believe you're envying me this dish. Try a little.'

'Please don't treat me like a baby, sir. I've told you I'm not hungry.'

'Then why do you look so envious as I enjoy the turbot?'

'I am not looking envious!'

'Peckish, then.'

'*Peckish?*' She was about to object vigorously, then caught the upturn of his lips. He was teasing her! She frowned,

80

then felt a gurgle in her throat, and despite herself began to laugh. 'Peckish?' she repeated. 'That is not a word to use of a young lady, sir! A young lady may feel inclined for a little sustenance, but she can never be peckish!'

'I stand corrected. But if this particular young lady would agree to try the turbot, or even the cold ham, I should feel less like feeding time at the bear pit!'

'Very well,' she agreed, 'just to keep you company.' The truth was that, surprisingly enough, she *was* hungry.

They ate in companionable silence for a few minutes. Maldon poured wine for her, and as she picked up her glass he raised his own.

'A toast,' he proposed. 'To the clearing of your father's name.'

'Amen.' She held up her glass, then sipped. 'You believe it can be done?'

'Of course.'

'But how?'

'By finding out who it was who did indeed kill Beau Gramont.'

'But who could have done it, Mr. Maldon? Beau Gramont was a very popular man.'

'So you say. But, forgive me, Miss Tyrell, men hear more of the truth than can be known to women. In the coffee-houses and taverns it was widely said that many a husband had reason to hate Beau Gramont.'

Hesitating, Amy nodded. After a moment's unwillingness she said: 'My own mother believes that Papa killed Beau Gramont in a jealous rage.'

'And did he?'

'Of course not! My father has too much sense to think Beau ever looked at Mama except as a neighbour and hostess who needed to be flattered a little.'

'So it appears that your father had little reason to harm the man. But there are others who might have done it.'

'Who, Mr. Maldon?'

'The men who are so anxious to have your father hanged for it—the Pegmen. Isn't it widely rumoured that landowners have to fall in with the smugglers' wishes? Lend them wagons and carts, horses and cattle, give them barns and outhouses in which to house their goods? Then why can we not assume that Mr. Gramont fell into their bad books in some way over such an issue?'

'Beau Gramont? In league with the Pegmen?' Amy frowned and shook her head. 'I think not. He was too ... too ...'

'Frivolous?'

'Perhaps that's the word. Too frivolous. I don't believe the Pegmen would ever have trusted Mr. Gramont with any of their secrets.'

Mr. Maldon sipped his wine. After a moment he remarked: 'Mr. Gramont lived very well.'

'Why, yes.'

'Imported Italian curios, including the dagger with which he was killed.'

'Yes.'

'Dressed his wife and daughters in silk.'

'Ye-es.'

'From what source did he draw his income, do you know?'

She gazed at him, perplexed. 'I've no idea.'

'Bernard played cards and lost money heavily. It's the talk of the coffee-houses that he has debts.'

'Indeed?' She watched him. 'And what else, sir?'

Mr. Maldon didn't tell her what else he

had heard of Bernard's escapades. Instead he said, 'Such things cost money.'

'Are you saying you think the Gramonts got their income from smuggling?'

'Miss Tyrell, smuggling is a business, much like any other except that it is illegal. In every business there is a man who lays out money in the first place. In smuggling such a man is known as the venturer—he ventures his money to buy silks and tobacco and spirits and tea without paying the duty on them. How if Mr. Gramont was a venturer?'

'You seem to know a good deal about it, sir?'

'Oh, aye,' he said in a nonchalant tone, 'one picks up such things in tavern talk.' He held up his glass to the light, watching the red glow of the candle flame through the wine. 'One of the riding officers, a smart fellow called David Bartholomew, has told me one or two things about the situation on the Hampshire coast.'

'Bartholomew?' she said. 'Uncle Pierce mentioned him.'

'Did he, now? It may be, Miss Tyrell, that Mr. Pierce's mind has gone along the same lines.'

She nodded, thoughtful. 'The difference is that you are willing to pursue that line of inquiry whereas Uncle Pierce shied away from it!'

'Mr. Pierce has known Beau Gramont and his family a good many years,' Maldon pointed out. 'He is unwilling to think of them as being friends of the Pegmen, perhaps.'

'Perhaps,' she said in a dry tone. 'Or perhaps it is just as he said to me—he is afraid. Whereas you are not, Mr. Maldon.'

He laughed and pushed the glass bowl of syllabub towards her. 'Come,' he said, 'let's gluttonise with a large helping of pudding and then get some rest. In the morning, Miss Tyrell, you are to buy your Papa some clean linen, some soap and other small items of which I made a list, then I will take them to him in the prison. I've made arrangements for him to be moved to a private cell, not by any means a luxurious place but better than where I found him. The warden is a decent man, I hear, an old soldier called Colonel McMurray. He will hand on to your father any personal necessities that you supply, and see that he receives food from outside the walls if you will make arrangements to pay for it. So we have much to do in the morning.'

Seeing that he didn't wish to talk about his own part in the affair, Amy said no more. After they had finished their meal they shook hands and parted. She went upstairs to bed, suddenly nearly overwhelmed with fatigue to the extent that she had difficulty getting out of her gown and into her night things.

The sheets on the bed were not as fine as those in her room at the Manor House, but they and the bed hangings smelt of starch and lavender. She lay breathing in the scent and thinking that Mr. Maldon, when he bent over her hand, had smelt of leather and plain soap.

Mr. Maldon. Jeffrey. Jeffrey Maldon. This evening, early in their conversation, he had momentarily startled her by using her first name. She had meant to rebuke him for the familiarity, but the moment had gone by. Now she wondered at it. It seemed to imply that he thought of her as Amy. She tried to think of him as Jeffrey, and the idea was not strange, not displeasing. Jeffrey Maldon, her friend.

Of course she could never feel towards him as she did towards Bernard. He was not as handsome, and he could be rather stern in a way that disconcerted her; whereas Bernard was always amusing and lighthearted. Or at least, that was how Bernard used to be, before the tragedy of his father's death. What was Bernard like now? Why did he never send any word to her?

She felt once again that desperate welling up of perplexity and grief, but she was too tired to cry. Gradually consciousness drifted from her.

Her last thought as she fell asleep was that Mr. Maldon had a good share of altruism in his make-up—because if he cleared her father of the charge of murdering Beau Gramont, he also cleared the way for a reconciliation between herself and Bernard.

Let it be so, she prayed, slipping into dreams. Oh, let it be so …

CHAPTER 4

As Mr. Maldon had foretold, the early part of next morning was spent in making the purchases asked for by Amy's father. Then she had to submit to being left in anxiety and frustration at the George Inn while Maldon carried the packages to Mr. Tyrell.

The waiting time was broken up by the reappearance of Bryce, looking shamefaced. 'Mr. Maldon told me I should come and ask your pardon, miss,' he said. 'I didn't mean to run away yesterday, but, my faith, Miss Tyrell, they were so enraged against you! I've never seen the like!'

'Nor I,' Amy commented. 'I wonder why they should have been in such a passion at me. What have I ever done to them?'

' 'Twasn't you, miss. 'Twas your father.'

'Certainly, I understand that,' she said. 'But my father was taken into custody for a crime that can surely have little interest to the citizens of Winchester?'

'Well, y'see, Miss Tyrell, those weren't exactly the good citizens of this town … I spent the evening keeping myself to myself in one of the taverns and I heard enough to let me know that about half of those men shaking their fists at your coach were friends of the Pegmen.'

'Do you say so? But, even so, Bryce, I should have thought that though they recognised the carriage with my father's initials, they would not have troubled themselves over it. What threat am I to them? A daughter visiting her father in prison?'

'Oh, they've had a setback to stir them up, miss,' Bryce said, anxious to win approval that might wipe out his failure of yesterday. 'The *Swift,* privateer, captured the *Three Brothers,* a smuggler's craft, day before yesterday. Four thousand pounds of tea and about forty casks of rum and brandy, to say nothing of coffee, silk and lace.'

'What! There's a cargo for you!'

'Aye, truly. 'Tis a great loss to them to have it taken by a government boat. So they are angry, and wishful to take it out on someone—and there you were, miss, riding into Winchester with hardly anybody to keep you safe. I don't care to think what might have happened if Mr. Maldon hadn't galloped up.'

'Nor do I, Bryce!' She thought with regret of some of the hard words she had uttered last night, and so as to change the subject went on, 'And so what has happened to this great haul of tea and brandy and so forth? Why don't the Pegmen go and get it back, rather than taking out their spite on me?'

'Well, you see, Miss Tyrell, it's locked up in Poole Custom House. They're dog-mad about it. If it had been piled up on a quay or a harbour wall with a couple of militiamen to guard it, they might have got it back easy enough. But a Custom House with padlocks on the doors, that's a different kettle of fish. And to make matters worse, the dragoons are out in the countryside today. That seems to mean that the government were kept informed of the *Swift's* activities and knew they'd need the army out to keep order. I dare say the Pegmen feel that for the first time there's some sort of real pother waiting for them. And rightly they deserve it,' Bryce ended, going red with indignation, 'raising their hands against a lady like yourself, Miss Tyrell ...'

Bryce then went off to have the coach put-to.

When Mr. Maldon walked in, he brought a carefully folded paper for Amy. It was a letter from her father, very brief but breathing love and concern in every word. Folded within it was another for her mother; Amy blinked back the tears as she put both notes lovingly away in the bosom of her gown.

'How was he, sir? How did he look?'

'Better, I think. He acknowledged to me that he had his first full night's sleep since being put in the gaol.'

They stayed only for a late breakfast of coffee and fresh bread before they set off for Markledon. Poor Bryce, totally untrained as a coachman, was very happy to have Jeffrey Maldon take his place from time to time on the box as they approached the more difficult stretches of road, which to Amy was a reassurance although she missed his companionship at the carriage door. He jogged along at the side of the vehicle on the powerful black, seemingly giving no care to directing the beast.

She said to him at one point, 'What would you do if your mount took fright?'

'Gylo? He has more sense than do so while he and I are together.' He laughed, bending down to look in at her. 'Don't be afraid, Miss Tyrell. No angry smugglers are likely to threaten us today. Have you not noticed the distant escort?'

'No, sir—where?'

'A quarter of a mile away on the heath ... five dragoons under a sergeant.'

'Did you ask for an escort, Mr. Malon?'

'When I heard the troops were out, I thought it a good idea. It's true I was able to rout the opposition yesterday, but then I took them by surprise. This morning, surprise might have been on *their* side. So a little precaution seemed called for.'

She was impressed. Here was a very quick and far-seeing mind at work. She began to feel hopeful, even, that he would find some way to save her father.

At the Manor House, Amy's mother fell upon her neck. 'My love!' she wept. 'I have been beside myself with anxiety! The most *horrid* rumours have been flying here—'

'There, there, Mama,' Amy soothed, with a glance over her head at Mr. Maldon that begged his forgiveness of this poor welcome. 'Everything is all right—'

'Now that you are back, yes, I'm more at rest,' Mrs. Tyrell gasped. 'But have you heard that the Pegmen are out in bands fighting and marauding? Because of some misfortune they have had—'

'We heard, Mama, we heard. Come, let's go and sit down. Don't you see I have brought a visitor with me?'

Mrs. Tyrell disengaged herself from Amy and raised a tear-stained face to Mr. Maldon. 'Why, sir, how kind of you to come calling!' she faltered. 'You are the very first ...'

'Mama,' Amy said, to remind her mother of the duties of hospitality, 'let me quickly tell you how wonderfully kind Mr. Maldon has been. He has agreed to take on the defence of my father and indeed has already visited him twice Look, he brought a letter from him this very morning!'

She held out the paper. Her mother took it as if it was alight and in flames, with great caution. 'From your father?' she whispered. From her face it might have been thought she had heard a voice from the grave. 'Oh, Amy! How did he look?'

'I didn't see him, Mama. He sent word by Mr. Maldon that he would prefer me not to come. But ask Mr. Maldon for news while I run to the kitchen in hopes of getting a meal on the table—'

'Nay, Miss Tyrell, pray don't,' Mr. Maldon put in. 'I shall not stay, if you'll forgive me.'

'But sir—it's the least we can do, to offer you some—'

'I must get about on business, ma'am. Too long has gone by and nothing attempted. It's a week now since Mr. Gramont was murdered, and who knows what has happened to any witnesses?'

'You mean Stephen Boles, I take it? Where can you hope to find him, Mr. Maldon, and at this time of night?' Amy found herself loath to part with Mr. Maldon even in such a good cause.

'Well, ma'am, I certainly shan't find him here at the Manor House,' he replied with faint impatience.

'Even if you find him,' Mrs. Tyrell lamented, 'he will only tell you what he said in court—that he saw Mr. Tyrell in a rage.'

'But perhaps I can make him admit that was a lie.'

'No, sir, it was the truth, I'm sure,' she insisted. 'Mr. Tyrell did not come to bed until late that night, and when he did he was very angry and disturbed.'

'Did he tell you why?'

'Oh no, I was half asleep—but I could tell by his breathing and the way he tossed about.'

'So although it seems clear that he went out that night, there's only Stephen Boles's word that he was at Parall.'

'But ... but ... I'm sure he was there, taxing Beau with his feelings for me.'

Maldon exchanged a brief glance with Amy. He read in her face what he himself sensed—that Mrs. Tyrell was romancing about the relationship that had existed between herself and her handsome neighbour.

'Had your husband any grounds for taking the matter seriously?' he said with complete bluntness. 'Had you taken any steps to embark on an affair with Mr. Gramont? Had secret messages passed between you that he might have intercepted? Did you keep assignations with him?'

'Mr. Maldon!' She was deeply shocked. 'I am a respectable married woman!'

'So there was nothing to force your husband to action.'

'But George has always had a violent temper.'

'That is a different matter from being a violent man.'

'But he could act rashly. He dismissed Stephen Boles on the spot.'

'He did not, however, take a stick to Stephen Boles. Would you expect Mr. Tyrell to take a dagger to a man who teased you and made you laugh?'

Mrs. Tyrell clasped and unclasped her hands. 'Who knows what a jealous man will do?' she murmured.

Mr. Maldon took his leave, thanking

his lucky stars that though Amy took her good looks from her mother, she inherited her good sense from her father.

He had already thought out where he was likely to get word of the chief witness against Mr. Tyrell. Boles the dismissed footman had gone to beg a bed at Parall, so Maldon rode up the drive and, though no groom came to take his horse, knocked on the door.

No answer.

He knocked again, more vehemently. After a long delay the bolts were drawn and the Gramonts' butler, Canoway, appeared in the doorway.

'Yes, sir?'

'I should like to come in, if you please,' Maldon said in surprise.

'Mrs. Gramont is seeing no one.'

'I have come to see Mr. Gramont.'

'Mr. Gramont is dead.'

'I mean, of course, the young Mr. Gramont,' Maldon said in the face of this assumed obtuseness.

'Mr. Bernard is not seeing anyone.'

'Please tell him it is extremely important, Canoway.'

'I'm sorry, sir. My orders are to admit

no one on any pretext.'

'Then tell me where I can find Stephen Boles.'

'Boles?' Canoway said, his long face going frozen with surprise.

'The former footman at the Manor House.'

'What do you want with him?'

Maldon saw no reason not to tell him. 'I am preparing the defence for Mr. Tyrell and I need to talk to Boles about his evidence at the inquest.'

'You're defending Mr. Tyrell?'

'Come, man,' Maldon said in annoyance, 'stop repeating what I say as if you were a trained starling! Where is Stephen Boles? Is he still here?'

'He's gone, sir,' Canoway said, backing into the hall. 'I've no idea where he's gone!'

Before Maldon could get another query out, the door had slammed shut.

Well, thought he, there's for you! What a panic to be in over a footman from the neighbouring household. What can be behind it?'

The rebuff only made him the more determined to get into Parall. He rode back down the drive, aware that he was being watched from behind the curtains of the morning room, and out into the lane. Here he tethered Gylo to a bush and walked back to the boundary hedge of Parall.

As he looked through the gaps in the hedge he saw a liveried footman walk down the drive and take up his stance at the gates. The man was shouldering a cudgel.

So it was as important as that to keep people out? An armed guard on the gates ...

Greatly intrigued, he remounted and rode away so that the footman could hear his departure. Once out of hearing he stopped again and went on foot round the estate, which was now masked by a high and handsome wall of red brick. It proved no great obstacle to a man as tall and as active as Mr. Maldon.

On the other side he found a rather tangled shrubbery, where a gravel path wound among the bushes. He kept off the gravel because of the sound it would make under his riding boots. The light was failing now; cloud had come up during the earlier part of the evening and now the added depth of twilight cast shadows over everything. By walking along the grassy edge of the path he reached a sheet of ornamental water, embellished with fountains, statues and a Chinese bridge.

Now he had to leave the shelter of the bushes to cross an expanse of lawn. Beyond the lake, the house stood silent in the gathering darkness, its windows shuttered, almost as if it were abandoned. Good, he thought, no one about. He emerged from the shrubbery and began to make his way forward.

Then he heard the sound of a little door creaking open. Footsteps could be heard on the flagstoned court surrounding the house. A cloaked figure was coming towards the lake. From the light tap of the footsteps, it was a woman.

She drifted in an undecided, aimless way along the far edge. Something about her began to alarm Jeffrey Maldon. She was not moving like a lady out to enjoy the evening air—to him she seemed more like some sad little ghost.

She spoke, and he recognised the voice.

It was Mrs. Gramont.

'You won't have long to wait, my dearest. I am coming—a wife's place is with her husband, is it not? But they're foolish ... foolish! *He* is like you, my love—when he tells me to do a thing I must obey, so I stay indoors and I think of you. But just this once I must go against his wishes, because I know you want me with you.'

It was a low babble of sound, almost incoherent. Why, thought Maldon, she is out of her poor senses! She was wandering along the verge of the lake now, staring into darkening waters as if she could see her husband's face reflected there alongside her own.

'He will be angry that I have come out. You were never angry, my own one. You smiled all the time. Ah, you smiled too much! And at too many people. You should have smiled only at me, and then nothing would ever have gone wrong between us.' She leaned forward, perilously close to the waters, her hands thrown out. 'Wait for me, my handsome John! I am coming!'

Maldon waited for no more. He

shouted in warning and ran to reach her, round the edge of the long pool of water, his riding boots pounding on the gravel walk. Mrs. Gramont, startled, wheeled at his approach. As he saw that she was distracted from whatever act had been in her mind a moment ago, he slowed.

'Good evening, Mrs. Gramont,' he said rather breathlessly, but trying for a conversational tone.

She peered at him. 'Who are you? What are you doing here?'

'Jeffrey Maldon, at your service, ma'am. I've come to offer my condolences.'

That phrase was a mistake. 'Condolences?' she repeated. 'No need for that. Everything will soon be well. John and I will soon be together.'

'Nay, now,' he replied, taking her arm in a gentle grasp, 'this is not the time for thoughts like that. Your son and your daughters need you. Come, let's go indoors to find them.'

'I don't want to see them,' she countered, almost querulous.

'You love your children, don't you?'

'Only Bernard,' she said simply. 'He

is like his father.'

'Then let us go in and find him,' Maldon said, and walked with her towards the house.

It was too much to hope that all this would have escaped notice. A little light-shod woman might walk about in the grounds without attracting attention, but a tall man shouting and running was bound to bring someone out to find out what was going on.

A man had come from the same little side door through which Mrs. Gramont had emerged, and was now hurrying across the lawn to them. As he drew near, Mr. Maldon could see that it was Bernard Gramont.

'Maldon!' he exclaimed, in utter astonishment. 'What-a-devil are you doing here?'

'Bringing your mother indoors from a delirious venture,' he said. 'You ought to take better care of her, Gramont.'

'Mind your own confounded business,' Bernard said, putting an arm round the frail shoulders of his mother. 'I told Canoway not to let you in!'

'Nor he did,' Maldon agreed. 'I climbed

the wall.'

'That is trespass, sir—'

'I admit it. If you wish to, you may sue me. But I need to speak to Stephen Boles.'

'He is not here, sir. And I wish *you* were not!'

'Come, Gramont, be reasonable. Miss Tyrell has entrusted her father's case to me, and so I—'

'Aye, well done, sir!' Bernard Gramont burst out. 'You may hoodwink Amy but you don't hoodwink me! I see you for what you are—an adventurer, and an unscrupulous one at that. She wouldn't look at you before, but now you think you'll get her all to yourself. Well, we'll see, we'll see, my clever friend!'

'Well-a-day,' Maldon said in surprise. 'How you hate me! But why? What have I ever done to you?'

'I never trusted you,' the other man replied, his voice rising almost hysterically. 'What brought you to this part of the world? To make a beginning as a lawyer? Nonsense! There are far more lucrative places to practise law. I saw through you from the outset. I knew you wanted Amy!'

'And why does that anger you so? *You* didn't want her.'

That brought Bernard Gramont up short. His fine-skinned, pale face went blank with surprise. 'What makes you say that?'

'By all that's holy—! Because you didn't take her, man! There she was, the prettiest and liveliest girl in the southern counties, and what did you do? You played cards, you chased the ladies of pleasure in Southampton and Poole—oh, aye, it was common talk. If you had cared sixpence for Miss Tyrell you would have spared her that humiliation.'

'You have no right to discuss Miss Tyrell's affairs.'

'More right than you have, Gramont. I am trying to help her father, whereas you, so far as I can see, are trying to impede the course of justice. Why won't you tell me where I can find Stephen Boles?'

'If you're so clever,' sneered Bernard, 'find him for yourself!'

'I will, believe me,' said Maldon, tight-lipped. 'But it would be a kindness to Amy and her father if you would put me on the track of the man who accused him.'

'Bernard,' Mrs. Gramont said suddenly, 'is Mr. Tyrell in some trouble?'

'No, no, Mama,' said her son, 'nothing of any importance. Come now, come indoors. You shall have some mulled wine and Janet will read you to sleep.'

'Nay, dearest, don't make me go to bed,' she said in a piteous tone. 'I have such terrible dreams! I dream that your Papa is dead, Bernard.'

Without another word to Maldon her son led her away.

CHAPTER 5

Next morning Amy Tyrell was on the watch for the arrival of Mr. Maldon. When she heard the sound of hooves on the drive she darted to the window of the morning room, leaving her mother in the midst of a sentence. But, alas, it was Mr. Pierce she saw being helped down from his fat little mare.

'Well, my dear,' he said as she was shown in, 'how are you? You went to Winchester, I hear. I hope you did not find the journey too exhausting. And my dear Mrs Tyrell—pray, ma'am, don't disturb yourself.'

But Mrs. Tyrell, in a flood of welcoming tears, was rushing towards him. 'Mr. Pierce, dear old friend!' she cried. 'So you have come to call! Ah, it's so good of you! Do you know, not a soul has been near us, save Mr. Maldon?'

'It's of Mr. Maldon that I wish to talk,'

the old man said, subsiding gratefully into a chair. 'He came to see me last night.'

'Did he? Oh, you wish to talk of business, do you? Then I'll go and tell Molly to make some refreshment,' Mrs. Tyrell said. 'We have no servants, you know, Mr. Pierce—'tis so tiresome! One has to go on foot and ask for things in the kitchen.'

She hurried out, and Mr. Pierce made no attempt to stop her. His faded old eyes were on Amy, and she had a feeling that there was something weighty on his mind.

'Child,' he said, 'why did you not ask your father to turn to me?'

'Sir?'

'On a matter of business—good heavens, he and I have been friends this twenty years or more. Why trust a man we none of us know?'

'Uncle Pierce,' Amy said with the beginnings of anger, 'Mr. Malden volunteered to take charge of the defence of my father—'

'I'm not speaking of the defence, Amy. True, I give you that—no one else would undertake it and Maldon put himself forward. But the other matter is different.'

'What other matter? What are we speaking of?' she demanded, anger giving way to mystification.

'You mean your father didn't discuss it with you first?'

'I did not see my father, sir.'

'What? But you went to Winchester ...'

'Aye, but met Mr. Maldon there, most fortunately. He undertook my visit to my father in the prison first, for he felt it would overset him if I arrived unannounced.'

'But you just said that you didn't go?'

'In the event, no. My father sent word that he would prefer it if I did not visit him.'

'Did he so?' the old man said, pulling at his lower lip.

'Why, yes, sir. He told Mr. Maldon to give me that message.'

'You only have Mr. Maldon's word for that.'

Amy stared, and felt herself colour up in indignation. 'Mr. Pierce, pray take care what you say! I don't believe Mr. Maldon would tell me something that was not true.'

Edward Pierce shrugged himself a

little more comfortably into the chair 'Tut, tut, don't be tetchy with me, little one. I'm your old Uncle Pierce, remember? I only wish you well. If I speak doubtingly of Mr. Maldon it's because I see more to doubt than you do. For instance, I now learn that you did not see your father at all, so you had no opportunity to express an opinion on his course of action until too late. But surely you must have been surprised when you saw the document?'

'What document, sir?' She hesitated. 'Do you mean the letter he brought me from the prison? I cannot say I was surprised by that—I was grateful, rather.'

'Nay,' said Mr. Pierce. 'Do you mean you have not seen it?'

'Seen what, sir?'

'The power-of-attorney.'

She blinked. 'P-power-of-attorney?' she stammered.

'He did not show it to you? Well, no matter—'tis much like any other. But what did you feel when you heard of it?'

'I ... I ...'

The old man suddenly sat up straight. 'You have not heard of it!' he exclaimed.

'No, sir. I can't say I have. But then ... Mr. Maldon had little opportunity ...'

'Fiddle-de-dee! He could have made an opportunity! Do you mean to tell me he didn't inform you that your father had given him power-of-attorney over his affairs?'

Her thoughts racing, Amy tried to grasp at her self-control. 'He has not told me thus far, Mr. Pierce, but I am expecting him soon and have no doubt he will make me *au fait* with all business matters—' She heard her own voice babble and cut herself off. She mustn't allow herself to sound as if she were in a panic.

Mr. Pierce sighed. 'I wonder at you, Amy! You are an intelligent girl—how can you deceive yourself so? You know as well as I do that you and your mother are now in a very strange situation—in the guardianship of a man you scarcely know, and without prior consultation on that point, either! Your father must have been out of his mind to be talked into such a thing.'

Amy drew a deep breath. 'It is not so strange, neither,' she protested. 'My father felt he must make some provision

for the running of his estates, and Mr.
Maldon had come like an angel of
mercy—'

'Angel of mercy!' Mr. Pierce echoed
derisively. 'Soldier of fortune, more like!
Come, child, look at it coolly. Your
father is in great distress, under threat of
hanging. Jeffrey Maldon reads of the
events in the London papers and comes
post-haste down to Hampshire to see
what he can make of his chances—'

'No, sir, that is unjust! He came to
offer his services.'

'Out of sheer goodness of heart?'

'Well ... perhaps not entirely. I believe
he once did intend to ... to offer for my
hand.'

'Ah.'

'But he didn't do so, sir, because he
had heard that I was pledged to Bernard.
He left for London on business—'

'Aye, and what happened to that business? He simply abandoned it, did he, to
rush to your father's aid? Now, Amy, use
your wits. He read that your father was
arrested and on a charge of killing Beau
Gramont, reasoned that that would have
broken up any marriage planned between

you and Bernard, and came to see what he could scavenge from among the pieces.'

'Uncle Pierce, I assure you, you are being most unjust!' she cried. 'He interposed between myself and a mob of ruffians in Winchester, at some danger to himself—'

'Truly? He rode up like a knight errant, did he?'

'Well, you may mock, but indeed he did.' She recalled that moment, and how his arms had gone about her as he helped her from the carriage. How grateful she had been!

'And how do you know he did not set the ruffians on you in the first place, so as to appear as a hero when he rescued you?'

'Uncle Pierce!' she exclaimed, aghast. 'That is really too much to accuse! I do assure you that I was in fear of the men, and he could well have been hurt when he intervened.'

'Mm ...' the old man said. 'Well, I retract that suspicion. But the fact remains that he prevented you from going to see your father, went in your stead, and

113

came away from the interview with a power-of-attorney that effectively puts him in charge of your father's wealth.'

'I can understand that my father might feel it necessary—'

'Nonsense! He was talked into it! Maldon is backing a double certainty. He hopes to marry you and lay his hands on the money in that way, but if by any chance you should refuse him, he will have control of the Tyrell lands—'

'That is not so. The estate will return to my father's control when he is cleared of this charge.'

Mr. Pierce let a long moment of silence go by. Then he said, 'But don't you see, Amy, that he does not think your father will be cleared?'

Amy sprang up from her chair. 'You are not to say that! Mr. Maldon will save my father!'

'And how will he do that, pray?'

'He will find out who really killed Mr. Gramont.'

'Will he so? In the face of a barrier of silence from all who wish your father dead?'

'He will save Papa!' Amy cried, clenching her fists. 'He told me he would!'

The old man struggled out of his chair and came to put his arms round her. 'There, there,' he said. 'Poor little girl, I understand how it is that you put your trust in him. You had no one else to turn to—yes, yes, I understand. But face up to it, Amy. Mr. Maldon would be taking his life in his hands if he tried to make inquiries on this matter. The Pegmen have made it clear that your father is doomed. Anyone who interfered would be a fool—and Jeffrey Maldon is no fool! He will do nothing—there is, in fact, nothing to be done. You have put your trust in a man who will take advantage of you, my dear.'

'No, no, you don't know him!' she cried, struggling with sobs that threatened to close up her throat. 'He is brave and good—'

'Amy,' Uncle Pierce interrupted, 'think about it. If he should be able by some miracle to clear your father, that would mean that the way was clear for you and Bernard again. That's so, is it not?'

'Yes, but—'

'Are you really telling me that this

penniless young man is going to spend his time proving your father innocent so as to hand you over at the end to his rival? No one is so altruistic, my love. I have lived seventy years and never seen such a one.'

'You ... you are wrong,' she faltered. 'Mr. Maldon and I spoke of Bernard. He understands my feelings on that score.'

'Understands? You told him that if your father were proved innocent you would hope to marry Bernard still?'

'It wasn't put into so many words. Mr. Maldon said that Papa was grieving about the unhappiness he had caused me by separating me from Bernard, and asked me if my happiness depended on Bernard.'

'And you said that it did.'

'I ... I don't recall. But I remember that he nodded and said that it was as well to be aware of such stumbling-blocks.'

Uncle Pierce snorted. 'Ha! So Bernard is a stumbling-block! *That* does not sound very altruistic, Amy! I don't believe he will endanger himself or put himself to much trouble when it's clearly to his advantage to wait for a clear field.'

'But your estimation of him is wrong, Uncle Pierce! How can I make you understand that he is not acting out of self-interest?'

'And how can I make you understand that he is not going to act at all? He will not do anything that would seriously alter the course of events. He may prate about action, but he will do nothing.'

'No, sir, he is going to find Stephen Boles and—'

'Faith, what good will that do? Even if he finds him, Boles will not change his story. If it is true—and it may be, Amy!'—he can't change it. And if it's a lie, Boles dare not change it. The Pegmen will make sure he sticks to the same tale.'

'Mr. Maldon says that he feels the truth has something to do with the Pegmen.'

'He may be right. But having said that, there's an end of it. Mr. Maldon will not succeed where the Excisemen and the militia have failed. Do you truly expect him to take on the Pegmen single-handed?'

That stopped Amy in her tracks. She saw all at once how much she had expected—how much she had taken for granted—from Jeffrey Maldon. Uncle Pierce was right: Mr. Maldon had no real chance against odds like that. How could she have been so silly as to believe in him? And yet … and yet …

'I see how you feel about it,' the old man said with great gentleness. 'You don't wish to give up the illusion of hope. The man told you a lie you wished to believe—'tis only human that you should cling to it. But now that I have told you of the trick he played—'

'Trick?'

'In getting your father to sign a power-of-attorney.'

'Oh yes. Yes, that was … that was kept from me. I see now that he may have had a reason for preventing me from seeing Papa. Although, Uncle Pierce, if Papa had told me what he intended, I should have agreed with it.'

'Quite so. It's the underhandedness of the act that makes it suspect. I hope it has brought you to your senses, child.'

Amy put both hands up to her face as if to smooth away the expression of despair forming there. 'But what am I to do, Uncle Pierce? My father has made

Mr. Maldon his lawyer and signed over his affairs to him. To whom else can I turn?' She hesitated. 'Will you act for me?'

'There's nothing I can do, Amy. In law Maldon has control. What you must do is keep an eye on him. Don't do anything on his advice without first consulting me. At least in that way we can ensue that he gains no further ground.'

'I suppose you are right.'

'Depend on it, I know what I'm doing. I'm an old man, my love, I've seen rascals as plausible as Jeffrey Maldon in my time. I'll see he does no damage.'

'But what I need is someone who will do some good! Can you see to it that he carries out the investigation that he promised?' She saw him look dubious and went on quickly, 'Pray undertake this, Uncle Pierce. I know you're not eager to go into danger, but if you have Mr. Maldon to go about asking the questions, you yourself can stay safely at home.'

This was not tactful, and the old man went red with irritation. Then he managed a laugh. 'Well, I'll try to make sure he does something,' he grunted, 'but if you want my opinion there's really nothing to be done. However, if you tell him I am keeping watch, it may cause him to take the thing more seriously.'

'Thank you, Uncle Pierce.'

Mrs. Tyrell returned then, with Molly bringing the tray, so that the painful conversation could be brought to an end. Mr. Pierce stayed only long enough to drink one cup of chocolate and then took his leave. Mrs. Tyrell, rather put out, settled down with the remains of the snack. Amy excused herself and went out for a walk in the grounds. She felt unable to chit-chat with her mother after what she had been told.

It was still quite early in the morning. As she wandered through her beloved herb garden she recalled the last time she had been at work there, when Jeffrey Maldon had come to speak to her. She went hot with embarrassment. Had she genuinely thought he had cared for her, had been hurt that she refused him? This matter of the power-of-attorney put him in a new light; he was after the money after all, like so many before him.

Oh, if only Bernard had spoken for

her! They might have been married by now and even these dreadful happenings would not have seemed so bad if she were Bernard's wife. She glanced at the tall box hedge that screened the lane across which the grounds of Parall began. So often, as a child, she had run across to play with Bernard and his sisters. She found herself moving almost unconsciously to the little wicket-gate through which her father had come that night, and before she had time to think about it she was slipping across the lane and going through the gap in the hedge that led to the rose garden of Parall.

Everything there seemed strange—it was as if a century had gone by since she had last seen these pergolas where the scented French roses bloomed in June. She heard her own footsteps on the paving stones, the swish of her skirts against a bench—and paused.

What was she doing here? This was the house of the dead man, the man they said her father had killed! She drew up, wheeled, and was about to hurry back the way she had come. But a voice spoke her name.

'Amy!'

It was Bernard, sitting in the shade of the rose arbour. He sprang to his feet. 'I didn't expect to see you here!'

'No—I'm sorry, I shouldn't have come. Forgive me, Bernard.'

They stood gazing at each other. She thought he was much paler than usual, although he had always had a clear, pale complexion. He was dressed rather carelessly—no brocades or fine lace, merely a lawn shirt and a pair of grey breeches.

'These are bad days for us, Amy,' he said, his voice hoarse.

'They are indeed.' She hesitated. 'How is your mother? You ... you never responded to any of my inquiries.'

'My mother is not well,' he sighed. 'And matters are not improved when your inquisitive lawyer comes here to harass her.'

'My lawyer?' she said. 'You mean Mr. Maldon has been here?'

'Oh aye, pretending to be busy about your affairs. Though how it can help matters to give my mother nightmares, I don't know.'

'Bernard, I swear to you, I had no

knowledge of this. It was not done with my approval.'

'That at least is something,' Bernard said. 'If you have any influence with him, tell him to keep away.'

'If I have influence with him?' she repeated, rather surprised at the phrase. 'Surely you know he has taken over the direction of my father's defence?'

'No, how should I know that?'

'But did he explain that? You said a moment ago, Bernard—"my lawyer".'

'I've heard rumours that you were seen in Winchester with him. It's unseemly, Amy. You know what will be said about it.'

'No, what?' she countered, a little annoyed. 'People say a great many things. They say my father murdered yours, but that is not true either.'

Bernard's dark eyes travelled over her, taking in the proud tilt of the head and the firm set of the mouth. 'Forgive me, Amy. I don't really know what to think these days. My mother is at the point of despair and my sisters don't know how to deal with her. The only one she will mind is myself. I have had scarcely a moment to think about ... to think about *us*.'

At once she felt a surge of protective pity. 'Dear Bernard,' she murmured, holding out a hand.

He came to her and took it. 'Oh, God, Amy, if you knew what I've been through!'

She might have replied that she too had had something to suffer; but all she said was, 'I know, I know,' as she touched his cheek with her fingers.

'It's all so senseless! It's wrecked our lives.'

'No, no, there may be something yet to be saved. Once my father's name is cleared—'

'But how is that to be done?'

'Mr. Maldon thinks the best way is to discover the real murderer.'

'But why must he come looking for him at *my* house?' Bernard exclaimed, looking haunted.

'Oh, I think he is on the track of Stephen Boles.'

'Stephen Boles left Parall immediately after the inquest, Amy. It's useless for Maldon to come here. Promise me you'll make him stay away.'

'Yes, Bernard dear, I promise.'

He took her hand up to his lips and kissed it with fervour. It was the most passionate kiss he had ever given her—a strange fact that troubled her as she took her way homeward a moment later. Janet, Bernard's sister, had come out to say their mother was asking for him; Bernard had hurried indoors and Janet, frowning, had stared at Amy and then turned away. Notably unwanted, Amy retraced her steps.

Her hand still carried the imprint of Bernard's kiss. She put the fingers of her other hand upon the spot. In all the time she had known Bernard he had given her some boyish hugs, one or two brotherly kisses on the cheek, and once in a game of blind man's buff had seized her round the waist and kissed her boisterously on the back of the neck.

But this strange salute of gratitude had had more genuine warmth in it than any of those. Gratitude? Was the most passionate feeling he could summon up for her merely gratitude because she promised to keep Mr. Maldon from worrying the family?

She sighed to herself. She had heard it said that in every love affair there is one who loves and one who receives love: it seemed that between herself and Bernard she was the giver of love. For a moment she was saddened; she almost rejected that role.

And then she thought: I've loved him for years, it's too late to change now.

Besides, he needed her. His sisters were no help to him in dealing with his grieving mother; but she, Amy Tyrell, could at least do something for him. She could tell Jeffrey Maldon to treat him with respect.

So Jeffrey Maldon, arriving at the Manor House a little after midday, found a chilly reception awaiting him.

She didn't even ask him to sit down. 'Where have you been all day, Mr. Maldon?' she inquired. 'I expected you here first thing in the morning.'

He frowned, and almost perceptibly drew back. 'I ask your pardon,' he said. 'I didn't know we had made an arrangement for me to come here early.'

'Naturally I expected you, since we

have still a great deal to discuss.'

'Well, that is certainly true,' he agreed, recovering himself. 'May I report to you on what I have been doing?'

'That is scarcely necessary. I have heard from others of your activities. The first thing I must tell you is that I absolutely forbid you to go to Parall again, where your presence yesterday caused a great deal of suffering.'

She saw the frown deepen between his brows. 'How did you hear of that?' he inquired.

'Bernard told me. I—'

'But I understood that you and Bernard had not spoken to one another since the tragedy?'

'I went to see him this morning.'

'Went to see him?'

'Why should that surprise you? Bernard Gramont is the man I intend to marry.'

She said it because she wanted to reassure herself, but once it was said she realised that it was something of a test for Jeffrey Maldon—if he reacted strongly against the statement it would lend credence to Uncle Pierce's view, that the man was a fortune-hunter anxious to capture her heart while she was parted from Bernard.

So she watched Mr. Maldon narrowly. But all she saw was a faint tightening of the lips.

'I am happy that you and he are on speaking terms again,' he said. 'I had the impression that these recent troubles had placed an impassable barrier between you.'

'Not the least impassable,' she said, very cool. 'I simply walked through the wicket-gate to Parall.'

'*You* went to *him,*' Maldon remarked. 'May I ask what impelled you to do so?'

She couldn't admit the truth—that she had gone because of an impulse to put the clock back, to visit Parall again as if she were a little girl with no deeper anxieties than whether Bernard would ask for the first dance at the ball.

So instead she said, 'It seemed time to take up old friendships again, particularly in view of news that Uncle Pierce had brought me—news that made me a little uncertain of new friends.'

She saw Mr. Maldon take a long, deep

breath. 'So,' he said. 'That is what this is about. The power-of-attorney.'

'Indeed, sir. The power-of-attorney.'

'I saw that Mr. Pierce did not like it last night when I showed it to him. He said one or two rather angry things to me.'

'And what did you reply to him, sir?'

'That he was at liberty to feel piqued if he wished, but the fact remains that someone must have the power to look after your father's business matters while he is unable to do so himself.'

'Very true.'

'Then why are you so angry with me about it?'

'I am not angry, sir. Angry? Why should I be angry? I am surprised and perturbed that you should do such a thing behind my back, but as to anger ... That argues a deeper feeling than is needed.'

Mr. Maldon walked to the window of the drawing-room and stood there for a moment or two, his back to her. The sunlight glinted on his fair hair, picked out the worn threads on his blue riding coat.

Amy thought, he does not powder his

hair because he can't afford to do so. His coat is worn because he is poor. These are the reasons that he is so quick to have my father sign away his rights to him. He can enrich himself in that way.

Yet somehow it seemed less likely than when Uncle Pierce had been explaining it to her.

'Sir,' she said uncertainly, 'if these matters are capable of another explanation, perhaps you could give it to me.'

He didn't speak for yet another moment. She had a dreadful feeling that he was going to walk out without another word. But at last he wheeled to face her. His steel-grey eyes were cold.

'Miss Tyrell, in this country it is usual for a man to be considered innocent until he is proved guilty. It would be a kindness if you would extend that same custom to me in this matter. You ask me to explain, but I have the feeling that to do so is to defend myself against an accusation of a much stronger charge. What exactly is it that I am supposed to have done?'

'Supposed to have done?' she countered, annoyed that for a moment she had been on the verge of weakening. 'Do you deny that you persuaded my father to give you his power-of-attorney?'

'I do indeed deny it! It was he himself who suggested it. My feeling was that he should send the document to Mr. Pierce asking him to act, but he replied that I was the only legal counsel who had taken the trouble to come to his aid, and he therefore begged me to undertake full charge of his affairs. If you doubt it, go and ask him.'

'Ah,' Amy cried, 'but you would not let me see him when I had the chance! First you forbade me to go, and then you came with a supposed message from him saying he did not wish me to come to—'

'A supposed message?' Maldon broke in. His voice was grim. 'Are you saying that I lied to you?'

'It certainly strikes me as remarkable that my father should have refused an opportunity to talk to me.'

'Then you have little understanding of how a man can feel,' he said. 'He wanted to spare you the misery of seeing him in such surroundings—he acted out of affection, out of generosity. But I begin to

131

think, Miss Tyrell, that you have no conception of either.'

Amy gasped. 'How dare you say such a thing, sir!'

'Oh, I dare! I have seen you at close quarters in these last two days, and your chief concern seems to be for your own self-importance.'

'That is not true! You have no right to say that! I am thinking only of my father!'

'And how does it help him to antagonise the only man who comes to his aid?'

'Ah, there you are, that's your trump card, is it not? You think you can do what you like, say what you like, because no one else will undertake the investigation. Well, Mr. Maldon, you are wrong. I can manage very well without you. I will do as much as you are likely to do, and perhaps more.'

'You?' he said, with scorn.

'Oh, don't sneer, sir! I can get advice from Uncle Pierce, and as to the finding of Stephen Boles I daresay I can manage that as well as you can.'

'You are talking nonsense. The Pegmen are antagonists much more ruthless than any of you have met at a whist party—'

'Do you take me for a fool? I understand that they are wicked men. But at least they are openly wicked—they make no pretence of friendship—'

'I see. You are saying that in offering my help I have only been pretending. What purpose would that serve for me?'

'You are the best judge of that, sir.'

'I begin to doubt that I am a judge of anything,' Maldon said with cold disdain. 'I took you for a good-hearted, intelligent girl, but I begin to see that you are as easily led as a tame sheep! Some cunning arguments from Mr. Pierce, a few complaints from that selfish idiot Gramont, and you are parted from common sense!'

'Bernard is not selfish!' cried Amy. 'He is hurt and unhappy—'

'He is silly and thoughtless, and always has been. He kept you dangling when any man in his right mind would have taken you in his arms—'

'Dangling?' Amy echoed, seizing on the only part of this that struck home. 'Your language is not very gentlemanly, Mr. Maldon!'

'No, but it is honest—and my honesty has been called in question. On grounds that you ought to dismiss at once, if you were any judge of character. Bernard Gramont was playing on your sympathy when he complained of my visit to Parall—if he had any real concern for you he would do all he could to help find Stephen Boles. And as for Edward Pierce—'

'Yes, what of Mr. Pierce? Belittle him if you can. He has been a friend of my father's since I was a tiny child.'

'Are you sure he is a friend? Might he not be fonder of your father's money than of his character? To be lawyer to George Tyrell, squire of Markledon, brings fine fat fees and high reputation—therefore to find that someone else has been given the power-of-attorney is bound to annoy him.'

'There is another side to that story, Mr. Maldon. To come to Markledon as a struggling young lawyer and find that old Mr. Pierce has all the clients worth having might be very irritating. So to be given the power-of-attorney over the biggest estates in the district is a great triumph.

But let me tell you, if you think to make your fortune through that, you will be disappointed. From now on I shall take charge of all my father's affairs. You are released from that task.'

Mr. Maldon drew himself up so that his tall figure positively loomed over her.

'You are not competent to discharge me, madam. Your father engaged me. Only he can give me my *congé*.'

She had a feeling that he was right. But she could drive home her point in a different way. 'Cling on to the semblance of usefulness if you must, Mr. Maldon. But you will not get a penny from doing so. I shall act for Papa, and I shall tell him I have done so if you present him with a bill. You will not receive any payment, and so I warn you.'

'Indeed?' said Mr. Maldon through his teeth. 'Then I had better exact my payment now, had I not?'

'What do you mean, sir?'

For answer he stepped up to her and before she had the least suspicion of what he intended, he had taken her in his arms.

He pulled her savagely against him and brought his mouth down on hers. There seemed to be no love in the kiss—and yet there was passion. Though she struggled, he held her fast. She could feel an unrelenting strength in the arms that bound her to him, and after a moment she let herself become passive. To fight against him was useless.

In that instant, when her body yielded to the fierceness of his embrace, the savagery vanished. His mouth upon hers was like silk on silk, the steel bands that had seized her were replaced by gentle caresses. Amy felt her heart lurch within her breast, and for one traitorous moment her fingers were longing to feel his soft fair hair under their touch.

But she stiffened and pulled herself away. He let her go.

'Well, sir,' she said in stifled voice, 'may we mark the account "Paid in Full"?'

If there had been a softening of his expression it was gone at those words.

'Oh no, Miss Tyrell,' he replied. 'That was only a first reckoning. The final bill will be presented when your father walks out of Winchester Gaol a free man—and on that day, beware, for I rate my services high!' 136

CHAPTER 6

A very angry man, Mr. Maldon strode out of the Manor House and threw himself on his horse. He went headlong down the drive, then turned at random across country at a gallop, seeking to vent his anger on some strenuous activity. If the big black was surprised at such treatment after the hardship of two days' travel, first from London and then from Winchester, he made no demur, but stretched out his neck and answered the pressure of the heels on his flanks.

But quite soon, after about a mile, his master drew rein.

'Nay, Gylo, good boy,' he said, leaning forward to pat the horse on the neck, 'I'm proving I'm a fool as well as a villain! What good does it do to tire you out, riding in the wrong direction? I should be heading back to Markledon, not careering about the country in a rage.'

Gylo blew through his nostrils and jerked his head a little, to let Maldon know he was listening.

'She will never like me now,' Maldon said. 'And I don't deserve that she should. But truly, her devotion to that self-indulgent fool Gramont is enough to put an angel out of patience—and I am no angel.'

Gylo gave a little snort.

'What? You think I am? But that's only because I see you well fed and carefully groomed, old friend. If it was as easy to prove to Amy Tyrell that I am an angel, heaven might soon open its doors to me.' He sighed. 'Well, it's no use regretting what is done'. And after a moment, in a lower tone, 'I don't even regret it! To hold her in my arms was worth almost anything!'

He turned Gylo and began to make his way home at a more reasonable pace. He had rooms in the house of an elderly couple just off the High Street of Markledon, where his landlady greeted him with, 'There's a man waiting for you in your office, Mr. Maldon.'

'A man? A client?'

'As to that, sir, I don't care to know,' Mrs. Mason said in a rather quavering voice. 'And I'd take it a favour, sir, if you'd make arrangements to move elsewhere.'

He paused in the act of tying Gylo's reins to the waiting-bar. 'Why so, Mrs Mason?' he asked, taken aback.

'Well, Mr. Maldon, sir, forgive me, it's nothing personal. A well-spoken gentleman you are, and no trouble as a lodger, but ... well ... it's been said that you could bring trouble here.'

'Ah! You've had threats from the Pegmen?'

'Sir, sir, I don't want to discuss it!' She put the corner of her apron up to her eyes. 'Mr. Mason and I aren't young, you know, and are not fit to deal with the likes of ... of ... well, sir, the long and the short of it is, you must go, and go at once.'

'But you must give me a month's notice, Mrs. Mason,' he replied, watching her as he spoke. 'That was our agreement—a month's notice on either side.'

'Nay, sir, I'll refund the rent you've paid, so long as you'll agree to go. I beg you sir, please don't stay out your notice.'

He took one of her plump little hands in his. 'What have they threatened, ma'am? Have they said they'll harm you?'

'They've told us,' she lowered her voice to a frightened whisper, 'they've told us they'll set fire to the house if we don't drive you out!'

So, he thought, he was that much of a danger to the Pegmen? His quick mind put two and two together. Here was reinforcement to his belief that Mr. Tyrell was innocent, that the charge of murder was merely a stratagem to get him out of the smugglers' way, that Stephen Boles was in the pay of the smugglers.

'I'll try to find somewhere to go,' he promised Mrs. Mason. Alas that he had quarrelled with Amy—if he had kept his temper he might have been able to stay at the Manor House now that he was about to become homeless.

He went into the ground floor room he used as an office. A man rose and confronted him, so suddenly that Maldon seized him by the lapels of his jacket to ward him off.

'Good for you, sir,' said an amused

voice. 'I see you're on your guard!'

'And who the devil are you?—Why, it's David Bartholomew, is it not?' And in fact, now that his eyes were accustomed to the dim light indoors, Jeffrey Maldon could make out a slight, trim figure in a dark coat and riding breeches, a thin and pointed face under dark hair beginning to recede. David Bartholomew looked shrewd and intelligent, too.

'Yes, Mr. Maldon, the riding officer for the Department of Customs and Excise, at your service. I hear you've been looking for me?'

'Aye, and damned elusive you've proved to be,' Maldon said, throwing his hat on his desk and gesturing the other to a chair. 'All this morning I've been riding about Markledon trying to discover your whereabouts.'

'Mr. Maldon, this is a good time for friends of Mr. Tyrell to lie low,' said the other man, sitting down rather wearily.

'So,' Maldon said, 'you're a friend of Mr. Tyrell's?'

'Say rather he's a friend to me. He's supported me in my work when others hereabouts would be happy to see me drown or disappear. I tell you, sir, the amount of control that the Pegmen have in this district is frightening—only Mr. Tyrell was prepared to try to bring them to justice, and gave suitable sentences to those I was able to catch with smuggled goods in their possession.'

'And that's why the Pegmen are so particularly anxious to see George Tyrell hang?'

'Oh, there's more, Mr. Maldon. Y'see, the Excise and the Navy between them have no luck catching the smugglers. The government can't spare the men or the money. Although,' Bartholomew went on in a musing tone, with a sharp glance at his host, 'I do hear rumours that a special investigator is to be sent to the area, to see if he can learn something of what's going on, for instance among the gentry. Us commoners can't mingle with the landowners and such, of course.'

Maldon gave a shrug. 'One would have thought that that would be confidential information, if it's true?'

'Aye, surely, but as I was hinting, there's people in high places who benefit from the smugglers' activities. No doubt someone in the London office has been paid to pass on hints of that kind. And it may not be true, of course.'

'Quite so,' Maldon agreed. 'But Mr. Tyrell is not one of the landowners you suspect of being involved?'

'On the contrary, sir,' the exciseman said with approval. 'Mr. Tyrell himself paid for the hire of a ship and crew, a privateer called the *Swift*—'

'Ah!' exclaimed Maldon.

'Aye, so you've heard? They took a big contraband cargo just the other day, from a yawl, the *Three Brothers*. And the Pegmen are furiously angry about it.'

'But how could it be known that Mr. Tyrell had put up the money for the privateer? Surely that was a secret?'

'He told no one but me, sir,' Bartholomew said in a sad tone, 'yet somehow they got wind of it. I reckon it was through that footman, Stephen Boles—listening at keyholes or going through his master's papers on the sly!'

Maldon rubbed his chin thoughtfully. 'So then he passed on the information to his masters—but who? Who gives orders to such as Stephen Boles?'

'That's what we've got to find out, Mr. Maldon. Seems to me it might be someone in the Gramont household, because when Mr. Tyrell threw him out Boles went straight to the Gramonts.'

'Well, I tried making inquiries there, and had the door closed in my face. When I got in by rather underhanded methods, Mr. Gramont evaded giving me any answers to my questions.' He pondered. 'It seems beyond doubt that Mr. Tyrell and Beau Gramont had an angry scene the night Beau Gramont died. What do you think it was about, Bartholomew?'

The exciseman frowned. 'Difficult to say, sir. Mr. Tyrell's temper takes fire easy, as you might say. But two things in particular would set him off. One is his daughter—and truly, sir, 'tis shameful how the young Mr. Gramont behaved, considering he was expected to marry Miss Tyrell.'

'Aye,' Maldon said in a grim tone.

'And the t'other is the smuggling. Mr. Tyrell believes that defiance of the law is turning this whole district into a wilderness where honest men needs must obey scoundrels. If Mr. Tyrell had an argument with Mr. Gramont, it could well have been about either of those two things.'

'I wish he would tell me,' Maldon muttered. 'I did my utmost to persuade him, but he refused to speak of it.'

'Don't that make you think, sir, that it was something to do with Miss Amy? He loves her dearly. He wouldn't want to say anything to harm her.'

'I must go back to Winchester,' Maldon decided. 'I *must* make him confide in me. While I am away, David, will you try to find this man Boles? You would probably have more success than I could, because you know more about the haunts of the smugglers.'

'That's true enough, Mr. Maldon. And I think it's likely I'll run him down in Poole.'

'Poole?'

'Aye, sir, 'tis odd indeed, but there seems to be a general drift in the direction of Poole these last few days. I don't understand it myself.'

Maldon thought about it. 'Can it be anything to do with the captured contraband? I remember Bryce told us that it had been locked up in the Custom House at Poole.'

'So it has, but then what? They can't get it out. I suppose they're moving in that direction just to see what happens to their goods.'

'I wonder if that's the reason?' Maldon remarked. 'It might not be a bad notion, David, to let the London headquarters know that the Pegmen are showing an interest in Poole.'

'You think so, sir?'

'It can do no harm.'

'But what could they do, even if they knew? There's me and a couple of other officers—and I'm not even sure that both of *them* are honest men. And there's a platoon of dragoon soldiers, but they're spread thin all over Canford Heath from their barracks in Christchurch.'

'If you make it sound urgent enough, David, you might get a naval frigate to act as watch-dog.'

'Indeed, sir? You wouldn't like to suggest who I should inform as to get a result like that?'

Maldon shrugged. 'The Paymaster-General, Mr. Pitt, is a man of influence.'

146

Bartholomew gasped. 'But I could scarcely write to Mr. Pitt, sir!'

Maldon looked down at him from his perch on the edge of his desk, studied him, and appeared to come to a decision. 'I will write a note,' he said, 'which you must include with the report you send. But you must promise not to mention this to anyone.'

'Trust me, sir.'

'Faith, I *am* trusting you,' said Jeffrey Maldon, 'and if word leaks out that I am sent here by William Pitt to clean up this mess of spying and dishonesty on the Channel coast, it will be disastrous. Prime Minister Pelham hates and is jealous of Mr. Pitt—one word that his rival is having an investigation carried out into the administration, and charges of intrigue and bad faith will be thrown about! It could cause a government to fall.'

'I appreciate the confidence you show in me,' Bartholomew said with great earnestness. 'If there's aught I can do in return ...?'

'Well, to be sure, there is something! I'm off to Winchester as soon as may be, but when I return I shall have nowhere to rest my head, like Elijah. Can you give me a bed?'

'Certainly, sir, but it's not much of a place.' Bartholomew was flattered to be asked and yet embarrassed.

'No matter.' Without more ado Maldon found a pen and began to write the required note for His Majesty's Paymaster-General.

Miss Tyrell was likewise writing a letter. As angry as Jeffrey Maldon when he left, she had snapped at her mother when that poor lady came downstairs in her best lace cap, intending to charm their guest.

'He's gone, Mama, so don't trouble to make any arrangements about a special dinner for him.'

'Gone? But … what a short visit! I thought he would stay to dinner. When will he be back?'

'Never, I imagine.'

'Never?' Mrs. Tyrell repeated faintly. 'What do you mean, never?'

'I have told him I don't wish to see him again. I would rather not explain further, ma'am.'

'Oh, if you meant that it embarrasses you to have him here after you have refused his offer of marriage, that's not important, Amy.'

'There's more than that, Mama. I learn that he talked Papa into signing a document—'

'A document?' her mother cried, alarmed. 'What kind of document? A confession?'

Amy came to her senses. It was utterly wrong to confuse and upset her mother, who never had a very strong grasp on practical matters. 'No, Mama dearest, of course it is not a confession,' she said with vehemence. 'Papa has nothing to confess to. You must believe that! He has done nothing wrong.'

'But if you have sent Mr. Maldon away,' moaned Mrs. Tyrell, 'who will prove it?'

Who indeed?

It took Amy half an hour to soothe away the alarm she had caused, and when that was done she sat down to think what she ought to do. She had behaved very badly—she saw that now. She had confronted Mr. Maldon with an accusation of deceit and dishonesty because Uncle Pierce had put it into her mind; but now that she came to consider it she realised that Uncle Pierce was likely to be jealous of Mr. Maldon's friendship with her father. She had been upset on Bernard's behalf. But after all, if Mr. Maldon was to learn anything about what happened on the fatal night, he must surely make inquiries at Parall, the scene of the crime.

When she came to review the quarrel she had just had, she had to admit that what had hurt and stung was the phrase Maldon had used—the one about being kept dangling by Bernard. After that she had completely lost track of logic; she had simply been lashing out at him to punish him for what he had said. She had wanted to make him feel as foolish and small as that phrase had made her feel. 'Kept dangling ...'

But it was true. She had had that thought herself more than once this summer, as the days went by and still Bernard didn't declare himself. The best time for a wedding in the country was the summer. If Bernard didn't ask for her hand before the end of September, the autumn rains

150

and the winter snows would make it impossible to have guests at the ceremony, and that meant putting it all off for another year. Another year! She would have been twenty-one by then and still unmarried ...

That was why it had hurt so much when Jeffrey put it into words, she admitted to herself. That was why she had been so cruel.

And then he ... he had taken his revenge ...

Well, of course, she would never, never speak to him again. Never. Even if he stood by what he said and refused to take her dismissal, she would never admit him to the house. Even if he succeeded in freeing her father from prison.

If he intended to do so, she reminded herself. According to Uncle Pierce it would be to Jeffrey Maldon's advantage for her father to stay where he was.

Yet somehow she couldn't believe that the indignant rejection of her charges had been mere acting. He had been deeply angry. She knew that was true, for her shoulders still felt the force of his fingers as he had seized her and pulled her towards him. Her lips still felt the imprint of his savage kiss.

His reaction had been genuine. Ungentlemanly, barbarous, wrong—all those things, yes. But genuine. He had kissed her out of a desire to punish her for the hurt she had inflicted.

This was a strange kind of logic, perhaps, but she found it convincing. And if it was true that she had hurt him by her accusations, didn't it then follow that her suspicions about him were wrong?

Yet there was the matter of talking her father into signing the power-of-attorney. Uncle Pierce was right when he said it was a way of profiting from the distress of the Tyrell family. It was the kind of thing a clever fortune-hunter might think of. And he certainly had not mentioned it at any time during the previous day, though they had spent twelve hours in each other's company.

True, there had been the difficulties of Bryce's poor driving to contend with, and the care of the carriage horses on the hard roads, and an argument with the innkeeper where they had stopped for refreshments. And when they reached home her mother had distracted his attention with her news of bands of Pegmen roving the neighbourhood, so that he had hurried away in hopes of finding the missing Stephen Boles.

She wished now that she had greeted him with less frigidity at midday. He might have had some explanation of his actions to offer. Now it was too late. The scene that had occurred—the angry accusations on her part and the cold savagery of his revenge—all that had made a barrier they could never cross.

All the same, she wished to know the truth about his power-of-attorney. So, since she was sending Bryce back to Winchester on a horse with some personal belongings of her father's, she sat down to write. She included the inquiry about the power-of-attorney in a gently teasing way, so as not to let Mr. Tyrell know what had happened.

'Uncle Pierce is put out that you have given such powers to a young whippersnapper like Mr. Maldon and begs to know whether he has lost your confidence? He is anxious in case you were persuaded into it while you were in distress and so, dearest Papa, a word of explanation that I could give to him would be a boon.'

When Bryce had been dispatched on the pack-pony with home-baked pasties and her father's favourite slippers, Amy wandered about the grounds in frustration. She wondered whether Mr. Maldon would be doing anything on her father's behalf and if so, what? The main thing was to find Stephen Boles. But according to the servants, Stephen Boles had disappeared from Markledon. No one seemed to know where he had gone.

She could go back to Parall, of course, and ask Bernard. But somehow she shrank from doing that. The old boy-and-girl affection seemed to have trickled away; now there was a strange distorted relationship between them, a feeling of protective love on her side, and on his, who knew what?

Who else would know the whereabouts of Stephen Boles? If she could not ask at Parall, where else could she inquire?

Then it came to her. Nancy! Stephen Boles's sweetheart, the girl for whom he had bought the silk shawl. He had swindled the household accounts out of some money to buy a shawl for one of the kitchen-maids out of the Manor House, but Nancy of course had fled with most of the other servants.

She hurried back indoors and rang for her maid. The faithful Molly hurried into her bedroom, half expecting to hear that Miss Tyrell had the vapours, for faith, 'twould be no wonder if she did, considering all that the poor soul had gone through these last few days!

'Molly,' Amy demanded, 'where has Nancy gone?'

'Nancy?'

'Nancy Saythe, the kitchen-maid.'

Poor lady, thought Molly, she's taken leave of her senses. Inquiring for a kitchen-maid, indeed!

'Now, now, miss, don't you worry your head about that,' she soothed. 'Best if you lie down and I'll bring you a posset—'

'Molly, pray don't talk to me as if I were a ninny! I want to find Nancy Saythe because she and Boles were handholding, were they not?'

'Why, that's quite true, Miss Tyrell!'

'So she may know where he is now, may she not? Therefore I want to speak to her. Where did she go when she got frightened away?'

'As to that, she said she was going to Miss Hilderoth in the village,' Molly said, looking doubtful. 'She sews nicely, does Nancy, for a kitchen-hand, but I doubt if she does it well enough for Miss Hilderoth to take her on.'

Miss Hilderoth was the local dressmaker, a very handsome young lady who had come from London to set up shop in Markledon. All the local ladies who could afford it had their gowns made by Sarah Hilderoth. If Amy had been about to be a bride, she would have ordered her wedding-dress from that establishment.

Certainly it sounded unlikely that Miss Hilderoth would take on Nancy Saythe, whose hands were rough from kitchen work and quite unfitted for the fine silks that were sewn in the workrooms there. Nevertheless, it would be worth inquiring; even if the dressmaker had sent her away, she might have some idea where Nancy had gone.

'I shall go there at once,' Amy announced.

'Nay, never say that, Miss Tyrell,' Molly gasped. 'You daren't show your face in Markledon at the moment, the feeling runs so high. One sight of you in the carriage and you'd have the mob around you—'

'Then I shan't take the carriage.'

'But, it's no better if you ride in, miss! They've only to see you and they'll—'

'Then they shan't see me. Or at least they shan't notice me, Molly! Come, we must find a way to change my appearance so that I don't look like Miss Tyrell of the Manor House. Let's see if we have anything sober and demure in the wardrobe.'

Molly was horrified, and more so when it was proved that even Amy's least expensive gown had the cut and finish of a lady's possession, so that it would be necessary to borrow a dress from the lady's maid.

'My dress, miss? You can't be serious?'

'Why not, Molly? We're about the same size and height, and if I brush the powder out of my hair and wear a plain cap, who is to know I'm not a simple country girl?'

Molly was one of the private opinion that her mistress could never look like a simple country girl, but nevertheless went to her little room in the attics and brought back her best clothes: a dark brown wool gown, a muslin kerchief edged with English crochet, grey thread stockings with white clocks, a brown cloak with a hood and a pair of French gloves once given her by a suitor. Amy refused the gloves but donned the rest, added a pair of thick leather shoes, and set off on foot for Markledon.

As she walked along the high road a man in a gig came trotting by from behind her. He slowed his pace a few yards ahead.

' 'Morning, sweetheart. Like a lift?' he called.

It was the landlord of the Garland. He hadn't recognised her, well though he knew her. She pulled the hood of the cloak yet further over her head and made a gesture of refusal, without speaking. He raised his whip in salute and went on.

Miss Hilderoth's shop was halfway

down the High Street. At the moment that Amy entered the village, Jeffrey Maldon was riding out at the other side to head for Winchester. Had she looked up, she would have seen that tall figure on the black horse moving steadily away towards the north, but she was concentrating on not appearing nervous as she mounted the two stone steps outside the dressmaker's and raised the door-knocker.

A girl of about fourteen opened to her. 'Tell your mistress I want her,' Amy said, without thinking that this wasn't the kind of language expected from a "simple country girl". The child, however, scurried away as bidden, and in a moment Sarah Hilderoth appeared from the back of the shop.

'Good afternoon, ma'am,' she said, and then stopped short.

They knew each other, of course. Amy had had two or three gowns made here. Miss Hilderoth stared at her but recovered quickly.

'Why, Miss Tyrell,' she said, 'what do you want here?'

It wasn't exactly impolite, but it was

certainly not the civility that Amy was accustomed to. She raised her eyebrows and, perhaps for the first time, really looked at Sarah Hilderoth.

She was a truly beautiful woman. Taller by a head than Amy, she seemed about two years older. Her skin had the sheen of a pearl and something of its colour—clear and translucent. She dressed extremely well by standards that Amy didn't admire—an abundance of lace, an over-elaborate hair-style, and many rings.

The odd thing was that she was very tense; she showed a particular animosity and anxiety.

'Miss Hilderoth, I've come to ask you if you have Nancy Saythe working for you?'

'Nancy? Yes, she's here. What do you want with her?'

'If you remember, she was in our employ. Most of our household staff have run away—where, I know not. But when I heard that Nancy might be here I thought I would ask her to come back.'

'You'll be wasting your time,' said Miss Hilderoth. 'No girl in her senses will go back to the Manor House.'

Amy controlled her temper in the face of this waspishness. 'Let me at least ask her,' she begged. 'We have almost no one to see to the kitchen ranges nor make the beds.'

'And of course you're too much a fine lady to do it yourself,' snapped Sarah Hilderoth. 'Very well, I'll send for her.' She rang a little silver bell, and the young girl appeared as if she had been crouching in terror behind the door. 'Fetch Nancy,' she commanded.

When she had gone Amy said in a conversational tone, 'I'm surprised that her work is of high enough quality for you to—'

'Leave me to mind my own business,' interrupted Miss Hilderoth, 'and you mind yours.'

'I'm sorry. I didn't mean to seem inquisitive.'

'No, it's simply that you can't get used to the notion that you've no importance or influence any more, without your father to lord it over everyone as landowner. Well, it was time you learnt your lesson.'

'I see,' Amy said, looking down to hide

her heightened colour. It was very hard to have to accept treatment of this kind, and particularly from a woman to whom she had always been quite polite when she had her dresses fitted. She was shocked and puzzled by the gratuitous rudeness with which she was being addressed.

The door from the back premises opened and the former kitchen-maid came in, a tall slender girl with fine eyes and a gentle expression.

'Why, Miss Tyrell! I couldn't believe it when Betty said—'

'How are you, Nancy? We have wondered how you were faring.'

'Oh, I'm surely grateful to you for your interest.'

'But not grateful enough to go back to the Manor House,' sneered the dressmaker.

'Is that why you've come, miss? I fear I—'

'Well, I did rather want to ask you something, Nancy. I very much need to speak to your sweetheart, Stephen Boles. Can you tell me where he's gone?'

'Stephen?' Nancy said in surprise.

'Nancy has nothing to say to you on

that score,' Sarah Hilderoth put in swiftly. 'You misled me, Miss Tyrell. You said you wished to speak to her about her employment.'

'I didn't say that was *all* I wanted to speak about—'

'As to Stephen, he's off to Poole Harbour, I'm thinking.'

'Be silent, girl! Didn't I just say you had nothing to tell her?'

'I'm sorry, Miss Hilderoth, but it didn't seem wrong to—'

'Whereabouts in Poole, Nancy?' Amy put in.

'Why, to one of the inns, I suppose.'

The door opened once again and a man came in, speaking as he walked. 'I heard the girls come down so I knew you'd got rid of her—'

He broke off. He and Amy stared at each other.

It was Bernard Gramont.

CHAPTER 7

How Amy got out of the place she could never afterwards remember. Embarrassment and pain blotted it all out of her mind. The next thing she knew she was walking fast down Markledon High Street with her cheeks flaming with distaste. She had forgotten to pull the hood around her face to hide her features, but no one hindered her or waylaid her. She reached the outskirts of the village, hurried on for another ten minutes, and then, finding her legs giving way beneath her, she sank down on a milestone.

She clasped her hands tightly in her lap and stared down at them. She didn't see them—what she saw was Bernard's face as he understood that she was still in the shop.

'I knew you'd got rid of her.'

He had been speaking about Amy. He had been skulking upstairs, waiting for her to leave. He would have been glad if she had been gone.

All at once a thousand things became clear to her. His unwillingness to ask for her hand in marriage, his shallow affection, even the excuses so often made for him by his family: 'Bernard will come later, he has business in Markledon.'

Business? Yes, business at the dressmaker's. An unlikely tale.

The fact that he was there today showed how important to him was the companionship of Sarah Hilderoth. Amy had seen him at Parall, seen how genuinely miserable he looked, and heard how his mother depended on him: so if he came all the way to the village to see Miss Hilderoth it argued a deep need.

Probably everyone in the neighbourhood knew. She felt certain that Mr. Maldon knew. Only Amy—poor blind fool—had been ignorant of the love affair between the son of Beau Gramont and the village dressmaker.

Well, now she knew. Now there was an end of all the longing for Bernard to declare himself, the forward-looking to a happy married life with him. All that was in the past. She understood what she should have sensed months ago, if she had not been so wilfully dense. Bernard didn't love her, probably never had. He had been fond of her, oh, yes—in the days of their childhood he had played with her and agreed that when they were grown up they would be married.

But he had grown out of it. She had not—not until now, in this one painful step of seeing their relationship in its adult aspect.

She sat for a long time on the milestone, hearing the traffic on the high road—a heavy trundling cart, packhorses, a light carriage with some young men of fashion who called to her to cheer her up and join them for supper. The shadows were lengthening. She must get home or her mother would be out of her mind with worry.

Both her mother and her maidservant were on the watch for her. Molly thought: 'Poor soul, how pale and tired she looks! How wearily she's walking!' Mrs. Tyrell thought: 'What on earth persuaded her to go into Markledon looking such a fright? It's really most unsuitable!' And

Amy spent a wretched evening trying to account for her activities without admitting that she had been to the house of the village dressmaker and there seen the man she loved, very much *chez lui*.

As a result she slept badly and rose late. For once Mrs. Tyrell was about before her, sitting on the edge of her chair in the breakfast-room with letters in her hand.

'Amy! What a slug-a-bed you are! Bryce has been back from Winchester this hour or more, and there's a letter for you from your Papa.'

'Back already? How good he is, Mama! He must have risen at the very first glimmer of dawn, to reach Markledon by now.'

'And so he should,' her mother said with surprise. 'Did he not rise from footboy to under-gardener in our service?'

'But, dearest Mama, no amount of wages can repay him for the kindness and devotion he—'

'Pooh,' interrupted Mrs. Tyrell, 'if he thinks of asking for an increase in wages, he need not trouble himself. Well, well? What does Papa say in his letter to you? I have read and re-read mine—he insists he is well but I'm sure his heart is breaking, as mine is!' Here she brought her handkerchief up to her reddened eyes, and her daughter took refuge in unfolding the paper on which her name was written in her father's scrawling hand.

He opened by thanking her for coming to Winchester, for sending the little luxuries by Bryce and for the speediness with which she had done so. He said he was well, and in good spirits. Then he went on:

'I am a little vexed, however, to learn that our good old Uncle Pierce should have troubled you over the matter of the power-of-attorney. When I at last persuaded Jeffrey Maldon to undertake this role I specifically asked him not to let you know unless it was necessary, for I feared it might alarm or distress you to think I was handing over my affairs to another, as if I thought I would not be able to deal with them myself. The fact is that there are business matters concerned with running the estate which must be dealt with: for example, I promised Farmer Emhurst to have his lower field drained before the autumn rains set in, and so someone must hire the men and set the work in motion, for I would not wish to fail in a promise to one of my tenant farmers.

'Jeffrey pointed out to me that our Uncle Pierce was the properest person to whom to delegate this work, And indeed, dearest daughter, had Mr. Pierce come to see me I should have discussed it with him. But when I asked Jeffrey to tell Mr. Pierce I needed him, he had to explain—with some embarrassment—that our good old friend feels some nervousness in being associated with our family just at present.

'You need not tell Uncle Pierce that this was the reason I turned to Jeffrey—it might hurt his feelings, and I should hate to do such a thing. Perhaps you could say that I am a little confused and un-happy—and indeed, my love, I *was* so, and I cannot tell you what it meant to me when Jeffrey walked in among that crowd of common criminals in the gaol and shook my hand! What a true friend we have found, Amy dear. Although I will admit he might be influenced by some feelings and hopes he has on a certain score— but there, I will not write further on that for fear of embarrassing you, knowing as I do how devoted you are to Bernard. Yet Jeffrey will be a tower of strength to you, I doubt not. Fondest love, Yr. absent but anxious Father.'

Amy read this with tears beginning to prick her eyes and ended with salt tear-drops on her cheeks.

'What is wrong?' her mother cried in dismay. 'Is he ill? Is it bad news?'

'Nay, ma'am,' she faltered, trying to get control of her voice, 'on the contrary, my father is well and thanks us for what we have done for his comfort so far. Take no notice of my crying, Mama—it's mere foolishness.'

'Let me see,' Mrs. Tyrell insisted, holding out her hand for the letter.

Amy was unwilling to give it to her, for there would be the almost impossible task of explaining to her what it was that Mr. Pierce had not been entrusted with, and why not, and how Farmer Emhurst's field could be drained, and why it was important to have it done before the autumn.

' 'Tis full of business, ma'am,' she said, holding it out, 'about hiring men for some work, and legal matters.'

'Oh, in that case, I shan't trouble to read it,' Mrs. Tyrell said, spreading out her own letter again. 'In what he writes to me, he speaks of the food as being better now that you've arranged for meals to be taken in from the inn. I wonder if they know how to roast crown of lamb? Your father does so enjoy a roast crown of lamb.'

Amy had a deep feeling of shame at the suspicions she had so quickly accepted over Mr. Maldon's actions. Mr. Pierce had come, complained a little and voiced his resentment over Jeffrey, and she had accepted all of it without giving him the benefit of any doubt. She recalled her father's phrases—'When I at last persuaded Jeffrey to undertake this ...' '*At last* persuaded' ... That implied it was not easily done, and that moreover it was her father's idea, not Jeffrey's. And then, 'I specifically asked him not to let you know'—here was the explanation of the secrecy of which Uncle Pierce had made so much. Jeffrey had not wanted to distress her—it was as simple as that.

'Jeffrey will be a tower of strength to you.' Would he? After the things she had said to him, and the angry reaction she had brought upon herself? Amy had never been kissed as Jeffrey Maldon had kissed her: could two people meet again after such a scene and be on ordinary terms of politeness? Could she go to him and apologise, beg him to be a help to her and her mother?

He had said he intended to carry on with the investigation into Beau Gramont's death in hopes of freeing her father, but would he really do so? She tried to envisage what she herself would do if she had been insulted and condemned in that way; she rather thought she would run away and hide, and never go near that person again, ever.

But perhaps Jeffrey was made of sterner stuff.

By and by, as she finished her second cup of breakfast coffee, it came to her that she ought to restore Jeffrey's reputation with Uncle Pierce. It was wrong to let her uncle think that Jeffrey had talked her father into signing the power-of-attorney, or that he intended to make a secret of it. She must let him know he was under a misapprehension there.

So when breakfast was over and she had dealt with some of the usual household problems, she murmured to her mother that she thought she would go into Markledon.

'But you were in Markledon yesterday,' Mrs. Tyrell protested. 'And it made you very mopish and miserable! I can't think why you want to go again.'

'I need to speak to Uncle Pierce,' she explained.

'Oh, as to that, I don't think we should go to *him,*' her mother cried. 'He should come to us, and I think less of him for giving us that courtesy only once since your father was taken from us. Our friends have treated us shamefully, Amy.'

'Not all of them, Mama. Jeffrey Maldon has not fled from us.'

'No-o. Although I expected him to come back again more quickly, or at least send messages. But he is young,' Mrs. Tyrell sighed, 'young for a lawyer—he has not Uncle Pierce's experience and ability.'

'Jeffrey may have something more important than experience,' Amy said with some asperity, 'and that is courage.'

'Courage? Oh, well, of course, it is brave of him to stand by us against the Pegmen, I admit, but he will be well paid, you know, Amy.'

'But he has not even discussed the matter of fees,' Amy replied, coming to that realisation for the first time. 'I don't think a word about money has passed Jeffrey's lips.'

'Amy,' her mother reproved, 'what is this strange idea of referring to Mr. Maldon by his first name?'

Amy went fiery red. 'I'm sorry, Mama,' she said, shocked at herself. 'But Papa refers to him as Jeffrey—'

'What your father does and what you may do are two entirely different things. I would advise you to be very careful over matters of propriety, situated as we are with the whole world ready to stare us down! And don't forget that you yourself dismissed him a short time ago as a fortune-hunter.'

'I did not, ma'am! I remember telling you I thought I had misjudged him on that point.'

'But you had thought it previously. And you know, one must admit it is very

174

strange that he should come rushing to our aid when no one else wishes to do so.'

'You are not holding it against him, ma'am? That he is brave enough to go against the tide and befriend us?'

'Well, no,' Mrs. Tyrell said, muddled by the complexity of her thoughts, 'but after all, dearest, if your Papa is hanged you will inherit a large fortune.'

'Mama!'

'It's no use crying out against it, Amy,' her mother said, dissolving into tears, 'the facts must be faced! Your father may be found guilty and you may be orphaned and I may be widowed—and we shall be targets for all the fortune-hunters in England.'

'You are not to speak so! It is wicked and self-centred and wrong! We must be strong in the belief that Papa will be set free, because if we think otherwise we weaken our own resolve to bring it about. Don't you see—'

'Wicked and self-centred?' Mrs. Tyrell sobbed, picking out the only words that mattered to her. 'You are calling your own mother wicked and self-centred? I never thought I should live to hear it—'

'I'm sorry, Mama—forgive me!'

But the emotional ravages of the scene took a long time to die down, needing the use of sal volatile and a darkened room; so the sun was past its zenith when Amy at last set out for the village.

She was riding Watcher, a spirited little pony her father had given her on her last birthday; she had perhaps had some hidden memory of how Jeffrey had dealt with the mob at Winchester by riding them aside with Gylo and felt that, if she met with any trouble in Markledon, she could use the same method. She certainly lacked the girlish eagerness that had prompted her yesterday to borrow Molly's clothes. If she was to face Uncle Pierce on behalf of Jeffrey Maldon, she preferred not to do it in fancy dress.

Why it should be so important to put the record right, she wasn't quite sure. It had something to do with justice, and something to do with a hidden hope that Jeffrey might hear of it and think better of her for it. She very much wanted the good opinion of Jeffrey Maldon.

Uncle Pierce's servant was very surprised when she handed him Watcher's reins and told him she wanted to speak to the lawyer. 'Sure, he's not expecting you?' he queried. 'He said to me only yesterday that for one reason or another he felt you and Mrs. Tyrell might be moving out of the Manor House to pleasanter quarters quite soon.'

'We have no intention of being chased out of our home, Datchett,' she replied with hauteur. 'Pray tell your master I am here.'

Mr. Pierce hobbled out of his office to greet her. 'Well, my dear, you have a great deal of courage,' he remarked as he allowed her to kiss his dry old cheek. 'Or should I call it rashness? You surely must have something important to discuss in coming here. About our dear Squire, I take it. Has he decided to plead guilty to the charge?'

'Plead guilty? My father? Uncle Pierce, how can you even think of it?' she cried. 'You surely don't think he *is* guilty?'

The old lawyer led her into his office and waved her to a chair. He himself settled painfully behind his cluttered desk. 'Well, to be candid, Amy—your father is capable of having done it.'

'Of killing a man? Never!'

'If the provocation was great enough, yes, he is capable of it. His temper has always been his greatest defect, and if a weapon happened to be at hand—'

'Nonsense! Weapons have been at hand before now when Papa lost his temper, but he has never used them. He's taken a stick to an impertinent urchin, I agree, but he has never used a sword—dear Uncle Pierce, my father has never even been involved in a duel!'

'Aye, aye, I see that you are a devoted daughter and don't wish to think ill of him.'

'I have heard from him, sir—I had a letter this morning in which he explains how it came about that Mr. Maldon accepted his power-of-attorney.'

'Indeed?'

'Yes, and it now appears that Papa had to persuade him into it.' She explained the situation, bearing in mind her father's concern not to hurt the feelings of their old friend. 'So you see, there was no question of anything underhanded. Papa was the one who put the idea forward, not Jeffrey.'

'Or should we rather say that that is what your father thinks?' countered Edward Pierce.

'I beg your pardon, sir?'

'My dear Amy, we all know people who are able to get their own way by means of letting other people persuade them into it. They protest, they hesitate—yet all the while they know what they want and they end up having it.'

'I think there is no reason to suspect Jeffrey of conduct of that kind', Amy objected. 'And you know, Papa did really tell him not to let me know of the power of attorney, so there was no wish to conceal anything from me for bad reasons.'

'Or did that young man perhaps put the idea into your father's head? "No need to tell Amy, it would only distress her"?'

'You are determined to think ill of him, sir,' Amy said, a sparkle of indignation coming into her eyes. 'I believe we must take my father's word for it that he knew what he was doing and saying. He is not yet in his dotage, Uncle Pierce.'

'No, but you yourself have just said that you think he hired Jeffrey Maldon because he was in some distress of mind.'

Amy was now in the difficult position of being unable to tell Uncle Pierce that her father's state of mind had been quite clear, and the story about being upset was only an invention to spare Mr. Pierce's feelings. She sighed and fell silent. The old man eyed her.

'You are very eager to think of Jeffrey Maldon as a knight errant,' he teased. 'Could it be that you are lonely and sad because you see nothing of Bernard these days?'

'Ah! I saw Bernard yesterday.'

'You did?' He raised bushy grey eyebrows. 'You went again to Parall?'

'No, sir.' She paused. 'How did you know I had been there a first time?'

'Bernard told me. We see each other quite frequently. I am the man of business for the Parall estate, you must know, Amy dear. Bernard told me you had been there and had been very kind and understanding. From that, I must say, I had assumed that you would be rather cool in your thinking about Mr. Maldon who, after all, has been harassing the family.'

'I don't think it can be called harassment to go to the house and ask for information—'

'But he climbed over a wall, Amy—was found trespassing!'

'Only because he could get no response by going to the front door.'

'Is that what he told you?'

'Uncle Pierce,' Amy said with sudden firmness, 'I should prefer not to discuss Jeffrey Maldon with you. I have the feeling that you took a dislike to him early on, and that you are prepared to think the worst of him in all circumstances. If I speak from my own experience of him, I have had only kindness and consideration—and therefore I may not sit by and let you suggest that he is untrustworthy. However, it was not that I wanted to mention just now. It was Bernard. I saw him yesterday, but not at Parall. No, not at Parall.'

'Where, then?'

'At … at Miss Hilderoth's shop.'

Uncle Pierce made a little exclamation of distress.

'Ah! So you knew about that?' she queried.

'About what? My dear Amy, there is nothing to know.'

'Come, I am not a baby, Uncle Pierce! He walked in as if he were very much at home there. It is clear he and Sarah Hilderoth have some sort of understanding. How long has it existed?'

'Nothing has existed, nor exists now, child! Don't fly off into a jealous miff.'

'Sir, I told you once—I am not a baby! This is not the time to talk of petty things like jealousy. I want to know—I need to know,' she urged, her voice breaking. 'I have spent almost all my life being in love with Bernard, and I need to know whether it has all been a waste of time.'

'Of course not. Sarah Hilderoth is not to be taken seriously, Amy! Beau Gramont would never permit it when he was alive, and you and Bernard would have been married very soon but for the tragedy. Now, however ...'

'Now, however,' she took it up, with some irony, 'Beau Gramont is dead and Bernard is master of his own intentions—and his intention seems to be to link himself with Sarah Hilderoth.'

'Nonsense! The owner of Parall cannot marry a dressmaker.'

'No, he is expected to marry the young

heiress next door and keep the pretty dressmaker in a separate establishment, is he not? Was that what Bernard had planned for us three?'

'My dear child, this is unseemly.'

'I agree with you! But it is not of my doing—I was the poor fool who went trustingly on, sure that Bernard loved me. And all the while he preferred Sarah Hilderoth.'

'I assure you his feeling for Sarah Hilderoth was never serious.'

'Serious or slight, it existed, and I never knew of it. I was kept dangling as Jeffrey so truly said.'

'No one regrets that more than Bernard, I am sure.'

'How can you talk such nonsense? He has no regrets. I tell you, I *saw* him. I heard what he said. 'Have you got rid of her?' he called—and he meant me. I was a nuisance, an intrusion. Sarah Hilderoth was the one he cared about. And he still cares for her. Oh, Uncle Pierce, why did you not tell me? Why did you let me go on and on expecting Bernard to ask for my hand?'

'But he would have done so, Amy, I

promise you. He spoke often of the time when he would settle down with you.'

'With a sigh, you mean. He thought of it as the end of his time of freedom. I wonder that he agreed to the idea when he could have insisted on having Sarah.'

'That would have been quite impossible. His father would not hear of it.'

'You mean that Bernard asked for permission to marry Sarah?'

'No, no, of course not.'

'That *is* what you meant! Oh, heavens,' Amy said, hiding her face in her hands, 'what an idiot I have been! All these years, idolising the boy who came like a fairy-tale prince into my life—and he preferred the seamstress for his wife. Well, at least I know now. I have woken up from my fairy-tale. Harsh reality has shown me the truth and I can almost feel it in me to be thankful, for if I had married Bernard and then learned afterwards that he had never loved me—'

'But he does love you, Amy!' Mr. Pierce broke in, in great agitation. He struggled out of his chair and came to her, to take her hand in both of his. 'This business about Sarah Hilderoth—it's a mere infatuation. He'll get over it. You and he were meant for each other—'

'No.' She shook her head.

'But you were, you are! Both your families wanted the match, your lands lie alongside each other, you would make such a perfect pair—'

'No, Uncle Pierce. It's finished. I would have been the happiest woman in the world a few weeks ago if Bernard had asked me to name the day, but now if he came to me I should refuse him. I know now that he has never loved me as a man should love the woman he marries—I know now that he never could.'

'Oh, you are overset by what has been happening, my dear—'

'No, it isn't that. I have learnt such a lot these past few days, Uncle Pierce!' Despite herself, she heard a piteous note in her own voice. 'I've learned that ... that there can't be something more between a man and a woman than fondness and companionship. There can be enmity, anger—perhaps even bitterness. But those at least make a standard of comparison for the tepid affection I have had from Bernard—they show its total lack of depth. If he never saw me again, Bernard would not grieve. He would say, "I wonder what ever happened to Amy Tyrrell?" and then turn the page of his newspaper. And I blame myself for an equal shallowness that must have existed in me, for not having known all this!'

'Tut tut, you are having a fit of the vapours about nothing, Amy! Just because you came upon Bernard in his little love-nest, you are breaking your heart. In a few days you'll have forgotten all about it.'

'Perhaps. But I shan't change my opinion about Bernard.'

'Are you so fickle, then? You can love him for as long as you have and change your mind overnight?'

'Fickle?' The word brought her up sharp. 'Perhaps I am. Perhaps I have been constant so long that when fickleness catches me, I surrender to it completely.' She gave a little laugh. 'At least no one can say I am a flirt. I was true to Bernard for my whole life up till now, and would have remained so for ever, even if we had never been able to come together after this tragic death. But I saw him with Sarah

Hilderoth, and everything is different. It's over, completely over.'

'So now eleven years of love are to be replaced by hate?' Mr. Pierce said with a sigh of reproach. 'Poor Bernard. Hasn't he trouble enough?'

'Who said I hate him? I'm fond of him—it's a habit I shan't grow out of, Uncle Pierce. I am fond of him and wish him well, but that is the end of it.'

'I'm happy to hear you haven't been swept up by jealousy and resentment. Depend upon it, Bernard needs you now more than he ever did. His family hang upon him like clinging shadows—his mother is very ill, poor lady. The death of his father has brought poor Bernard problems that he ought never to have had to face. I beg you, Amy, be kind to him.'

'Of course. Tell him he can rely on me to do all I can for him. Tell him I bear him no ill-will for yesterday's encounter.'

She kissed the old man in leave-taking. He held her back as she turned to the door. 'You will go straight home, Amy? It is really not safe to be about in Markledon alone.'

'I thought I might go to see Mr.

Maldon.' She was trying to screw up her courage for it.

'You'll be unlucky. He has gone.'

'Gone?'

'He was seen riding out of the village yesterday and is not back.'

She was disappointed and yet relieved. She wouldn't have to see him to apologise—yet she wished to see him. 'You keep informed of his whereabouts?'

'Oh ...' Uncle Pierce waved a gouty hand. 'In a place this size, everybody knows what everyone else is doing.'

The manservant handed her the reins of her pony but she couldn't mount straight away because a group of village boys, playing trap-ball in the broad main street, made Watcher restive. She led him, deep in thought.

The next moment she found herself immediately outside Jeffrey Maldon's lodgings just as he stepped out with his arms full of papers.

'Miss Tyrrell!'

She was so taken aback that she gave an exclamation and a little start, which caused Watcher to shy and prance a little, iron hooves ringing on the cobbles of the roadway. Mr. Maldon put his papers under one arm and with the other reached out to soothe the restless creature.

'There, there, my beauty. What a handsome boy it is. What is your name?'

'He's called Watcher, sir. I ... I'm surprised to see you, Mr. Maldon. I was informed you were out of Markledon.'

'As you can see, you were misinformed.' His tone was cool though polite. 'Is it wise to be in the village unescorted?'

'Perhaps not.But it seems strangely quiet today.'

'That's because most of the men are out, either marching towards Poole or watching those who are doing so.'

'Marching towards Poole? But why?'

'That is difficult to tell. May I help you to mount, Miss Tyrrell?'

'Well, I ... I should like a word with you, if it is convenient.'

'Not entirely. As you can see, I am moving office.' He took the papers from under his arm to show her. 'My landlady finds my tenancy unhealthy.'

'Oh, *sir!* That is on our account, is it not? I am so sorry.' She hesitated. 'And where are you moving to, if one may

189

inquire?'

'David Bartholomew, the riding officer for this area, has offered me accommodation in his cottage.'

'But that is some distance out of Markledon.'

'That matters little, since I seem not to have many clients in Markledon.'

'May I come with you to your new lodgings, so that we may talk?'

He shook his head. 'That would not be fitting. David's is a bachelor establishment.' He took a moment to think. 'May I ask you to wait one moment?'

'Certainly.'

He went back into the little house, and she heard him calling to his landlady for permission to bring her indoors.

'Nay, sir, I'd rather not!'

'Oh, come now, Mrs. Mason. Miss Tyrrell must be known to you. Surely you don't begrudge her a few minutes' shelter in your house?'

'But it's on account of her and her father that there's all this trouble,' Mrs. Mason faltered.

'Very well, I will take her to the Garland where they can scarcely refuse to serve us—but they will be very uncivil, I am sure.'

'Oh, Mr. Maldon ... I would not want anyone to be rude to Miss Tyrrell, sweet lady that she is. Well then, let her come in—but pray don't stay long, sir.'

He reappeared on the doorstep. 'Pray come in, Miss Tyrrell.' He hitched Watcher to the post that marked the little forecourt in front of the house. 'As you no doubt heard, we must not overstay our welcome.'

'Thank you.' She came in, her full-skirted riding habit brushing the sides of the narrow doorway. He showed her into a front room that had been his office, a spartan enough place. There was only one chair, which he placed for her.

'You wished to speak to me, ma'am?'

'Yes, sir. I ... I wrote to my father yesterday—'

'Yes, he told me he had had a letter.'

'You have seen my father, sir?' she cried.

'That was where I was when they told you I was out of Markledon. I rode to Winchester to clear up some important points with him.'

'And ... and he told you he had heard from me?'

He nodded.

'Did he tell you on what score?'

'No, he did not.'

'I wrote to ask him about the power-of-attorney, sir. And he explained it to me.'

'I see.'

'I scarcely know what to say next, Mr. Maldon. I am very, very sorry for having accused you so unjustly.'

'Thank you. I accept your apology.' He was standing a little in shadow, so that she could not properly make out his expression as he went on: 'I believe I owe you an apology also.'

'Yes, sir, I believe you do.'

'I make it now. I regret my actions on that occasion.'

'I accept your apology.' She held out her hand. 'Let us start afresh.'

He took her hand, and for one moment she thought he was going to carry it to his lips. But, to her surprising disappointment, he gave it a brief pressure and released it.

'Did you come to Markledon on purpose to say this to me?' he inquired.

'I ... I believe I did. I could not have been easy without this explanation, once I had a letter from Papa. Oh, pray, sir—how was my father? He writes that he is well—does he seem so?'

'Yes, Miss Tyrrell, he is tolerably well. We had a long talk.'

'What about?'

'About the reason for his strange refusal to speak about the events of that night. He said at the inquest that he had not been at Parall, although it seemed clear that this was untrue. That first time I saw him in prison I asked him for the truth, but he said that it was better to remain silent so that you and Bernard could take up your lives again.'

'Ah,' she said, on a note of pain. 'Bernard ...'

She saw him look at her. 'I'm sorry. But if you wish to know what I spoke of with your father, it may be necessary to grieve you further.'

'It was about Bernard, then?'

'I'm afraid so. I pointed out to your father that you and Bernard could never marry if he was convicted for the murder of Bernard's father. I told him point blank that since the tragedy Bernard had not come near you. He was very shocked at that. It seems he had taken it for granted that you and Bernard were still close.'

Amy bent her head so that her face was hidden. 'No,' she murmured, 'we are not close any more.'

'It may yet be possible to rectify all that,' he said in a steady voice. 'I am not sure that Bernard is involved. His father may have been lying.'

'His father? Lying? What do you mean, Mr. Maldon?'

'Beau Gramont told your father that Bernard is a ringleader of the Pegmen.'

CHAPTER 8

Amy's immediate reaction was a gasp of surprise and disagreement. 'Oh, no!'

'Please don't be distressed. It may be some cruel joke on the part of Beau Gramont, or some ruse to keep your father quiet. It isn't necessary to think ill of Bernard.'

'No—thank you—I was so startled—pray go on, sir.'

Truth to tell, her exclamation had a slightly different connotation from that which Jeffrey Maldon heard. She had been disclaiming the possibility of Bernard's being a ringleader in any enterprise. Much though she had loved him, and fond though she still was of him, she knew in her heart that Bernard could never lead anything. As to leading smugglers—planning devious undertakings, taking precautions against the Excisemen, organising the bestowal of the goods—all that was beyond him. The rough and cruel men who terrorised the district would never take orders from such as Bernard Gramont.

Jeffrey Maldon was quite unaware of the way her mind was working. He heard her cry out against what he had said and sighed inwardly. She loved him still … Incredible though it might be, she could still be hurt by a slur cast upon that self-centred booby. Well, he would try to tell the rest without causing her any more unhappiness than he must.

'I told your father with all the emphasis at my command that unless I knew what really happened that night, I could not hope to gain his acquittal. I said that if he was *not* acquitted, you and Bernard would be parted for ever.'

He paused to watch her. She nodded without speaking.

'When he had had a moment to think about it, he understood that I was right. Until then he had not imagined that … that Bernard would turn his back on you. I explained that to him by telling him how deeply Bernard's mother had been affected.'

'Yes, she is very ill, I hear.'

'In the end your father related to me the events of the night in question. He said that after dinner there was some discussion about measures against the Pegmen—do you recall it? I, of course, was not there.'

Amy cast her mind back. 'Nor was I, Mr. Maldon. I think there was talk of asking for more troops. Papa became cross about it, and I asked Bernard what had annoyed him. He said Papa thought it absurd to expect two hundred men to patrol the whole coastline of Hampshire and Dorset and that if there were more dragoons and—if I remember rightly— more cutters, the results would be greatly improved.'

'Did you know that your father had used his own funds to hire a privateer cutter and provision her?'

'No!' she exclaimed, astonished. 'Had he done so? It is so like him!'

'David Bartholomew told me—the *Swift,* to guard the waters between here and Guernsey, from which the Pegmen are making a regular run. No one except your father and David knew about it—the utmost secrecy was observed.'

'You may say so! I had no idea of it!'

'Exactly. So that when Beau Gramont made his clever pun on the cutter's name, your father knew that someone had had access to his private papers.'

'Why? What did Mr. Gramont say?'

'When your father stated that more cutters to patrol the waters would soon cut down the smuggling, Beau Gramont said: "The race is not always to the swift." '

Amy sat for a moment in silence. 'Yes,' she said slowly, 'I see. And afterwards Papa sat looking at him in the drawing-room with the strangest expression—of disbelief and reproach.'

'Well he might, Miss Tyrrell. Those two had been close friends for years, ever since the Gramonts bought Parall and moved in. All at once your father realised that for years Gramont had been making a fool of him, using him. Nothing he did as a magistrate to stop the smugglers was any good—his best friend was spying on him. He was very bitter about it when he told me, Amy. It had struck him to the heart.'

'I believe you,' she said, stricken. 'Poor

Papa! He always admired Beau Gramont—so much more handsome and witty and charming than he. And now to learn —or at least to suspect—that he was a double dealer ...'

'And all because the man could not resist the chance to make a *bon mot*. Your father said to me, ''I dare say he thought I was too stupid to understand the double meaning.'' But your father is not stupid, Amy. He had caught Stephen Boles out that very afternoon, buying tea at a low price from the smugglers and pocketing the difference for himself. And Stephen Boles, he tells me—'

'Came from Parall with a recommendation from Beau Gramont. He replaced a footman who was killed in a carriage accident about a year ago. And that footman', Amy said, thinking back, 'also came to us from Parall.'

'So Beau Gramont always had a spy in your house, you see.'

'It is insupportable!' Amy cried, jumping up. 'How dared they? Treat my father so, who is so good and honest and unsuspecting? Jeffrey, how could they?'

'Selfish men can do anything if they

feel it is to their advantage,' he replied, shaking his head at her. 'And though I only came to the district a short time ago, I had come to the conclusion that Beau Gramont was very selfish. He treated his wife very badly.'

'Flirting with other women, you mean? Yes, it made her very unhappy. But she adored him so, you know. We all did. He blinded us with his good looks and his fine clothes and his charm.' She paused. 'Yet you saw through him?'

'Well, perhaps that was because I came from outside, from London where men like Beau Gramont can be seen by the dozen in every theatre or gaming club. To me he was—' He broke off. He had been about to say: 'As trifling as his son.'

Amy was pursuing her own line of thought. 'So now we know why Papa went to Parall by the little gate that night.'

'Yes, he went to have it out with Gramont about the joke on the name of the patrol vessel.'

'And not, as Mama has almost persuaded herself, to challenge him for having flirted outrageously with her that evening.'

'No, I think not,' Jeffrey said, suppressing a smile. 'Your father has more sense than to think Beau Gramont was serious in that.'

Amy frowned. 'I should have disliked him for *that,*' she said with half a sigh. 'It was wrong of him, it made my father restless—and yet, you know, we all took it for granted that Beau Gramont could flirt with anyone's wife if he wanted to. Ah well, he will never make a husband uneasy again. So, Papa went to Parall.'

'He tells me he simply walked in by a side door you all used?'

'Yes, the garden room. It was always open, until very late—I think so that Beau could slip in quietly when he came from one of his little escapades.'

'Mr. Tyrrell walked in, and found Beau Gramont talking to Stephen Boles. If he had needed confirmation of his fears, he got it then.'

'Did they quarrel then, as Boles said in his evidence?'

'No, Gramont sent the footman off to the servants' quarters. When your father accused him, he tried to laugh it off. But when he saw that was no use he made a very bad mistake. He tried bribery.'

'Tried to bribe Papa?' Amy cried, aghast. 'He must have been mad!'

'He certainly was far less clever than people thought. It should have been clear to him that to offer money to a man like your father was an insult.'

'You are right,' she said, holding out her hand to him. 'Thank you for saying so, Jeffrey.'

He took her hand and drew her back to her chair. 'Sit down. There is not much more to tell, but it may distress you. When your father rejected any offer that Gramont could make, I suppose the man became frightened. A great deal of money is involved, after all—if Gramont had to take flight he would lose a fortune. And if he were caught, it meant hanging, or at the very least transportation for life.'

'Yes, I can see that. He had become very accustomed to a very fine way of living.'

'So I saw when first I came to the neighbourhood. I confess I was inquisitive enough to have a friend on 'Change make some inquiries, and was told that Beau Gramont had no investments to provide the kind of income he enjoyed.'

'So you are not surprised to hear that he was connected with the Pegmen?'

'No, almost not at all. Proving it, of course, would be a different matter.'

'And Bernard? You said at the outset that Bernard was implicated?'

'I understand your anxiety,' Jeffrey replied at once, 'and I'll try to set it at rest. I think that what Gramont said next can be discounted. He had tried ridicule, he had tried bribery—neither had worked. Now he tried to silence your father by telling him he would break your heart if he spoke out, because Bernard was in the business up to his ears.'

'But ... but it may be true, Jeffrey.'

'But it may not. Your father said they were shouting at each other in fury by this time. Gramont had reached a point where he needed to make sure that, in his anger, your father did not at once issue a warrant for his arrest. He had to say *something* to shake him. And he succeeded, for Mr. Tyrrell confessed to me that he could bear no more after that. He turned and walked out. That was when you saw him, I believe, walking home in the moonlight.'

'And when he left, Mr. Gramont was alive?'

'Alive and well. It becomes more and more important to find Stephen Boles. If he is one of the Pegmen and heard Mr. Gramont shouting out things about who was in the gang, he may have decided it was better to silence him.'

Amy stared at Jeffrey as he bent over her. 'Oh, sir ...' she said through stiff lips, 'if that is true of Stephen Boles, might it not equally be true of ... Bernard?'

For answer he knelt at her side and put an arm about her. 'Nay, Amy, don't allow yourself to think such things. I don't believe it. It is quite true, Bernard could be suspected just as your father was—but he is not a murderer.'

'No,' she agreed in a whisper, resting her head against his shoulder, feeling her throat close up with grief. 'I don't want to have to save my father's life by proving Bernard guilty of the crime. I should not like Bernard to have to suffer. He has been through enough.'

'Then we shall not let him suffer,' he told her soothingly, stroking her hair. 'There, don't be unhappy. I will do all I can to keep Bernard out of the case. David Bartholomew is trying to find Stephen Boles for me, and when he does, we will learn more—perhaps who are the other accomplices, for I can't believe Beau Gramont had the brains to run a gang like the Pegmen. There are others in this, there must be—and when we learn who they are we shall probably learn who is the real criminal. Meanwhile, trust me to do all I can to help Bernard.'

'I do trust you, Jeffrey,' she said on a stifled sob. 'I don't know what I should do without you. How kind you are! If you can clear my father and save Bernard from disgrace, I shall be grateful to you for the rest of my life.'

'Don't cry, Amy. I hate to see you cry. To me you have always seemed the epitome of all that is bright and brave and sparkling.'

'I've no brightness left, alas,' she said, burying her face against his coat. 'I think I'll never be happy again. Life can never be the same, can it? Everything will be changed even if we bring Papa safely home again. Even Bernard ...' She thought of all that had been lost and spoiled through what she now knew of Bernard, and the tears began to flow fast. After a second or two she managed with a great effort to gain control of herself and said with something like calmness: 'I have faced the fact that Bernard and I can never be married now.'

'But it may still be possible—'

'No, I have learned things now that ... that ...' She struggled for speech but some of the words were lost. All that Jeffrey heard was the name 'Hilderoth.'

'Ah,' he said. 'Who told you of that?'

'You knew?' She didn't dare look up as she asked.

'Yes. But then, men gossip amongst themselves, in clubs and coffee-houses. It means nothing.'

'You are trying to comfort me for having been a fool. Well, I've been cured of that, but not of wanting to see Bernard protected from harm. Pray, if you can, help him.'

'I'll do my best.'

'When I say that I shall be grateful, I

truly mean it, Jeffrey. My father is a rich man—'

'Come, now, you know better than to speak in that way.'

'I only want to assure you that ... that you shall have any reward that you ask for.'

He put a muscular hand under her chin and tilted her face up so that he could look into her eyes. 'Are you telling me that I can ask for Amy Tyrrell?'

'I think you were once on the verge of doing so, were you not? When you came to me that day in the herb garden.'

'But you had already given your heart to Bernard Gramont. And it is not easy to take back a heart that has been given away.'

'But Bernard doesn't want it,' she said, with a wistful shake of the head. 'And I thought that ... perhaps ... you did.'

'Come,' he said, 'we must go. Poor Mrs. Mason is probably on her knees outside the door praying that we'll soon remove ourselves.'

'Yes.' She rose, and stood for a moment staring up at him. 'Jeffrey ...?'

'Yes?'

'Will you do something for me?'

'You have only to ask.'

'Kiss me.'

'What?'

'Kiss me.'

He studied her. 'This is a strange request.'

'You did it once before without being invited.'

'And on that occasion I thought you did not much care for it.'

'Oh,' she burst out, 'I want so much to feel that I'm not a shadow, a nothing, a pawn in someone else's game! The life seems to have have been draining out of me, drop by drop, these past few days. I thought that if .. you would kiss me ... I might feel alive again.'

For answer he slipped an arm about her and drew her close. Then, with the utmost gentleness, he kissed her tear-stained cheeks, her eyelids, her brow, the line of her jaw and—finally—her mouth.

It wasn't at all like last time. That had been like a storm flash striking the granite of the mountain tops. This was like the blessing of sunlight on rain-dappled meadows, like the magic of a melody heard from far off, like the radiance of moonlight through a high window.

She gave herself up the bliss of his touch, feeling happiness and confidence running into her veins again. She was about to whisper some muffled endearment under his kisses when the door was flung open.

'Now, sir and madam!' said Mrs. Mason in high indignation. 'This is not proper at all, and I'll thank you to leave my house even if there's not a Pegman watching, for I'm a respectable married woman and I won't have such goings-on! I'm ashamed of you, Miss Tyrrell, you that I thought a lady!'

Scarlet with embarrassment, Amy hurried past the irate landlady with her face averted. Behind her she heard Jeffrey Maldon taking his leave.

'Mrs. Mason,' he said in a voice that was full of laughter, 'this was an occasion for which I'm willing to forfeit even your good opinion!'

CHAPTER 9

Next day was Michaelmas Day, on which the tenants were to bring their quarter's rents. Sixteen tenant farmers should have come, as well as some score of cottagers; but few appeared.

Farmer Emhurst was one of those who came. Not only that, he brought his wife and his two eldest children, to demonstrate past all doubt his loyalty to his landlord. 'How are you, Miss Tyrrell?'

'We are well, Farmer Emhurst, thank you. I see your family is flourishing.'

'Well enough, well enough.' He beamed on his son, a slender lad of sixteen who was beside himself with awe and embarrassment at being in the Manor House. 'And your dear mother? I hoped to see her.'

'So you shall—I hope you will take tea with us. But she is not accustomed to transacting business, Mr. Emhurst, and so she keeps to her room at present. Mr. Maldon here has been given charge of my father's affairs for the moment.'

'Ah, you're the young gen'leman that's trying to save the master, then? Sir, let me shake your hand. Anything I or my family can do—eh, Mother?'

'Quite so, Mr. Emhurst,' his wife approved. 'We have had so much kindness from the Squire that it would sit ill with us to fail in any way, if we can be useful.'

The farmer handed over a small linen purse in which coins jingled. Jeffrey counted the rent, found it correct, and penned a receipt. 'I'm afraid I have not had time yet to put in hand the work on your field drainage, Mr. Emhurst. Mr. Tyrrell instructed me to do so—'

'Did he though?' The farmer prodded his son with stubby fingers. 'There, Robin, I told 'ee he hadn't forgotten, though it would be small blame to him if he had, in the circumstances.'

'I'll see about hiring the men tomorrow or the next day—'

'Nay, Mr. Maldon, don't waste your time. There's none going to hire on to work for Mr. Tyrrell while the Pegmen are breathing threats against him.'

'What worries me more,' said Mrs. Emhurst in her forthright way, 'is how the Squire is ever to have a fair trial at the Assize Court? The Pegmen will "pack" the jury, just as they did at the inquest—a puppet-show, that was, as I said to Mr. Emhurst at the time.'

'It was one of the Pegmen as killed Mr. Gramont,' young Robin Emhurst burst out. 'Ten to one it was! They wanted him to take in some of their smuggled goods and he refused—I expect that was the way of it.'

'Have you seen any of the Pegmen near your farm?' Jeffrey inquired. The Emhursts had a stretch of land to the west, somewhat in the direction of Poole.

'Lord, yes, and bold as brass they are,' Mrs. Emhurst replied. 'Take my chickens without a by-your-leave, and no intention of paying a sixpence for them! I dursen't tax them with it, they're in such a touchy mood at the moment.'

'Indeed? And why is that?' Amy asked, feeling that from the safety of the Manor House she was somewhat cut off from what was going on in the countryside.

'It's because of the gunboat,' Jeffrey explained.

'Gunboat?'

'Yes, the Navy has sent a sloop of war, the *Nymph,* to patrol Poole Harbour and keep an eye on the Custom House. You know of course that a huge cargo of smuggled goods was seized by the Preventive men the day we came across each other in Winchester? It's now locked up in Poole Custom House and the Pegmen perhaps had some notion of taking it out. But not, I think, with a sloop of war on guard.'

'So there they are, milling about the countryside in a terrible bad temper,' Farmer Emhurst added. 'It's a powder-keg, you know. The least thing will set it off. So folks are nervous.'

'All the more credit to you for coming to us on Michaelmas Day, then,' Amy said. 'And now I'll go and fetch my mother to thank you for your visit.'

Although politeness demanded this, it was perhaps not a very good idea, because Farmer Emhurst's wife could not pretend she was hopeful about Mr. Tyrrell's predicament. Amy's mother grew more

213

and more depressed. Amy felt she could not do less than come out into the cool afternoon breeze to wave them off in their brightly painted cart, and Jeffrey gave her his arm.

As the fat old farmhorse plodded up the drive, a movement to the side caught Amy's eye. She turned her head. Bernard was standing on the inner side of the Manor House hedge, watching the scene as Amy waved goodbye from the doorstep. He must have come in through the old route of their childhood. Even as she saw him he turned and disappeared among the shrubs.

She had given a start of surprise, but when Jeffrey inquired the cause she shrugged it off. She didn't want to discuss Bernard with Jeffrey.

At an accounting that evening he came to the conclusion that he must go to collect the rents from those who had failed to appear—ten farmers and seven cottagers.

'Pray be careful, Jeffrey,' Amy begged. 'Perhaps it would be better not to pursue them just at present.'

'Nonsense. If we let it go, they will

think the estate is out of control.'

'Mr. Maldon, that is rather an unfeeling attitude,' Amy's mother objected. 'To be thinking about money while my husband's life is in danger—'

'Mrs. Tyrrell, ma'am, your husband will need money—ready money—to defray the expenses of his trial and so forth. It is no service to him to allow his business affairs to get in a tangle.'

Silenced, Mrs. Tyrrell withdrew into a huff. When Jeffrey had taken his leave she said to her daughter, 'That is rather a sharp young man!'

'Sharp, Mama? In what way?'

'In every way. Sharp of tongue and sharp of intellect. I am not accustomed to being put in my place quite so plainly.'

'He meant no incivility, I'm sure, ma'am. It's just that there is so much to think of—he doesn't have time to pay elegant courtesies in the way that Beau Gramont did, or Bernard.'

'Ah, Bernard ...' Her mother sighed. 'How one misses him and the company that used to come here. It is true Mr. Maldon is taller than Bernard, but he doesn't dress so well nor smile so much.'

That gentleman returned next day with some of the money owing to the Tyrrell estate and little to report otherwise. He was certainly not going to tell the two women that he had met with obstruction, fear, or downright rudeness in one or two of the farms he had visited, and had had the feeling as he rode that he was under constant observation.

'I must go to Winchester tomorrow,' he told them. 'I must report to Mr. Tyrrell about the business of the estate and ask for further instructions. Moreover, I have to see the clerk of the court and ask if a date has yet been set for the trial. I ought to find an advocate to take the case into court, if it ever gets so far—'

'Sir, I took it for granted that you would plead for my father,' Amy intervened.

'I think not. I am not a very eloquent speaker, as some recent experience has proved.'

Amy wasn't quite sure whether he was referring to some passage between themselves or to something in his own particular past. While she was thinking about it he went on: 'Shall you come with me to Winchester, Miss Tyrrell?'

'No, indeed, she will not!' her mother cried. 'We must think of propriety!'

'Yet I think Mr. Tyrrell would like a visit from his family, now that he is recovering his spirits and is in somewhat better lodgings there.'

'Very well, *I* will go,' said Mrs. Tyrrell.

'What?' It was a chorus of incredulity from her daughter and Jeffrey.

'Well, and why not, pray? If Mrs. Emhurst can come out from her farm to show the world she supports my husband, surely I can do as much or more?'

'But you will not like it, Mama,' Amy said. 'Prisons are unpleasant places—'

'Pooh, I know that! But after all, I shall not be in it above an hour, shall I? I can bear that. And Winchester is an interesting town, and truly 'tis dull here with nothing happening and no one visiting. I am very well able to face the event, I believe. And your father would be glad to see me, Amy.'

'Oh, ma'am—indeed he would!'

'Very well then, it's settled. You will accept me as a travelling companion, Mr. Maldon?'

'With the greatest pleasure,' Jeffrey said, his face giving away none of the consternation he was feeling at the prospects.

He had been looking forward to the chance of spending several uninterrupted hours with Amy on the journey. To have them snatched away was very hard to bear. Amy, too, was disappointed. She had not even been aware that the opportunity existed until Jeffrey mentioned it, but all at once it seemed unfair, unkind, that she couldn't go to Winchester with him. Then she was ashamed. Of course her mother must go. Although her father would be happy to see any member of his family, it was his wife he would be longing for.

Yet she had a hard time looking cheerful as the carriage was brought to the door next day.

'When shall you be back?' she asked, feeling already forlorn and bereft as Jeffrey took his leave.

'I think not until the day after tomorrow,' he said. 'We shall reach Winchester this afternoon and the rest of today will be taken up in visiting your father. Tomorrow I must go about among the

Assize staff, trying to learn who is to prosecute and when the judge is due to take the case. I daresay your Mama will want to be shown some of the silks and ribbons of the Winchester market too. So I think we must delay our return until the day after that.'

'I wish now that I had decided to come with you.'

'You can still change your mind.'

'No, I must stay with the servants. It is unfair to leave them here, guarding a house by themselves with angry smugglers roaming the countryside.'

'I trust you will remember that last phrase if anyone comes to the house. Pray don't open the door to anyone unless you know who it is.'

'I will be careful.'

'Amy, I wish I didn't have to go ...'

'I wish it too.'

'I'll be back as soon as I can.'

'I know.'

'*A bientôt.*' He touched his riding crop to the rim of his tricorne and turned Gylo towards the gates. The big carriage rolled forward ahead of him, the grinding of its iron wheels drowning out the words

Amy was saying in farewell.

She was rather glad of that afterwards, for what she had called was, 'I shall think of you all the time!'

The rest of the day seemed to go on for ever. Amy had never found time hang so heavy on her hands. She tried to busy herself with the tasks that were accumulating in a house needing a staff of fourteen and now looked after by a lady's maid, a butler, and a former under-gardener—she dusted, she made bread, she sharpened quills and filled the inkwells. But nothing seemed to dispel the great expanse of emptiness. For once she was glad to go to bed.

Next day bade fair to be as bad. But as she was sitting in the library dealing with some of her father's papers, Palmer the butler came in, his face alight with pleasure at the news he was bringing. 'Miss Amy, a visitor for you. Mr. Bernard is here!'

'Bernard?' she repeated stupidly, looking up. 'Here?'

'Yes, miss, shall I show him in?'

'Why—yes—please to do so.'

She put up her hands to her hair,

hastily brushed back this morning into a ribbon. She straightened the front of the plain little day gown she was wearing. That was all her preparation for receiving Bernard at last to the Manor House.

When he came in she thought he looked somewhat better than the last time she had seen him—at least, the last time she had had a real look at him. That moment in Miss Hilderoth's shop had been a mere glimpse; she had observed him closely last when she had gone to Parall and found him looking so wan and ill in the rose arbour.

'Good morning, Bernard,' she said with great calm, but without offering her hand.

'Good morning, Amy.' He took the chair she had indicated, stretching silk-stockinged legs in silver-buckled shoes on the old oak boards of the library.

'To what do I owe this honour? I rather thought you and I should never see each other again until, perhaps, the trial of my father.'

'Nay, Amy—don't be hard on me. I've come to ... to set things right about the other day.'

'The other day?' she said, feigning bewilderment.

'In Sarah Hilderoth's. You went off so rashly that I didn't have a chance to explain.'

'But you are going to do so now?'

'I don't know what you were thinking when you hurried off like that! I was only there because my mother sent me to inquire after her mourning clothes, which Miss Hilderoth is making.'

'Indeed? I should have thought your mother would send one of her daughters, not her son.'

'Well, you know she is a little astray in her head at the moment. We prefer not to cross her in any little whim. She asked me to go, and so I went.'

'I see,' Amy said, her voice showing the total lack of belief she felt. 'So your presence is explained—but not your words.'

'Words? What words?'

'You came into the room remarking that you'd come down because I'd been "got rid of"—'

'But Amy, my dear, I didn't know it was *you!* I'd fled upstairs when the maid went to answer the door, because I was ashamed for anyone to see me in a dressmaker's shop. When I heard all the girls coming downstairs I took it that the customer had gone and so I could take my leave. That's all.'

Was it true? Somehow she didn't think so. Uncle Pierce had made no demur when she had said there was a connection between Sarah Hilderoth and Bernard. But she didn't want to have a wrangle about it.

'If I misjudged you, I apologise,' she said. 'I may have misread the situation.'

'It hurt me, Amy,' he returned. 'I have enough to contend with at the moment without misunderstandings of that kind.'

She couldn't help remembering that when she had apologised to Jeffrey Maldon he had accepted at once, and returned an apology of his own. But Bernard felt he had nothing to apologise for, obviously. Perhaps he was right—but as to having enough to contend with, so had she, without having guilt heaped on her for being unjust to him.

Bernard was glancing about the room. 'How different it all looks,' he murmured. 'I feel as if I'm back here after an interval of many years.'

'Our lives are certainly so changed that a century might have gone by since you were last here.'

'And yet things go on much as usual. I saw the tenants coming in on quarter day.'

'Yes, I saw you observing us,' she said rather coolly.

'Oh, come, Amy, you can hardly blame me for feeling a curiosity to see how your knight errant was acquitting himself! I must say I was rather taken aback to see how assiduously he was taking control of the place.'

'My father has given him charge of his affairs for the time being. He has a high opinion of Mr. Maldon.'

'Naturally, a man would think well of another who appeared to be busying himself in his defence.'

'Appeared to be?' she interrupted. 'What do you mean by that? Mr. Maldon has been extremely—'

'Tell me what he has actually accomplished? He is seen walking about in Markledon, or riding about the country, but what good does it do your father?'

'He might have achieved more if you had allowed him to question the servants at Parall.'

'Amy, my household has been through enough! Besides, don't you think I have questioned them? If there was anything to be reported that could change the situation, I should have let you know it. But of course it makes a good excuse for Maldon if he can say I obstructed his enquiries.'

'How you dislike him!' she cried. 'I wonder why? What harm has he ever done you?'

He started to his feet. 'Dislike him?' he repeated, forcing a laugh. 'He is nothing to me! It's just that I hate to see you being fooled. You know, of course, that he boasted he would marry money soon after he came here?'

'What?' she gasped. 'How dare you say that! He is incapable of any such vulgarity!'

'Don't be absurd, Amy! Why have you let him bedazzle you like this? You were always so quick-witted before—'

'Ah, but that was when I was a happy,

carefree country heiress! Now I'm a sad little wretch with a father likely to be hanged for something he didn't do—and I am bedazzled, if that is the word you wish to use, because Jeffrey is the only shining light on my horizon. No one else came to our aid—only Jeffrey Maldon.'

'Because he sees a fortune in it, of course! Either you'll fall into his arms in gratitude if he frees your father or, if the worst happens, you'll wed him to have someone to look after the estates. Either way he wins—and you lose.'

'You have been talking to Uncle Pierce,' she said with disdain. 'He said some such nonsense to me.'

'It isn't nonsense, Amy. Uncle Pierce has had inquiries made about him, in London, where he came from. What brought him here in the first place? Don't you see he cast his eye down the list of heiresses that the fortune-hunters sell to each other, and decided you were a good catch?'

Amy knew of the lists that penniless young men made up from the news of legacies published in the newspapers. Many a foolish girl had been led to the altar by a man who wanted none of her but her fortune.

'You know, Amy ...' he sank his voice ... 'Uncle Pierce says he's reputed to be a Jacobite!'

'A Jacobite!' Amy knew nothing about politics but she'd heard her father fulminate about the rascals of two years ago who had followed the Young Pretender into England at the head of a pack of Highland brigands. A Jacobite! Enemies to King George, all penniless because their lands had been confiscated ...

She pulled herself together. 'There's no proof of that!'

'Uncle Pierce has proof. He's got a letter from a friend in London.'

'I shall never believe it till I hear it from Jeffrey's own lips.' After a moment of wild thought she added, 'And anyway I don't care! Papa would disapprove, but I don't care!'

'So it's as bad as that, is it? You're so much under his malign influence that—'

'Malign! How can you use such a word? He's done nothing but good and useful things here. I don't understand you, Bernard. Don't you want me to have a friend? Do you prefer that I should be absolutely alone, without helpers, in this fight to save Papa?'

That cut off the next words he was about to utter. He crossed the room and took one of her hands, though she tried to prevent it. 'Amy, you and I have been bound to each other by the closest of ties since we were children. You must know that I hate to think of you unhappy. Oh, this wretched, wretched murder! God knows my father didn't deserve to die, but neither does yours. Oh, Amy, it's such a dilemma!'

She was pained and embarrassed by his breakdown. She wanted to tell him that she was sorry for him but that she had not the strength to bear his woes as well as her own. Finally he turned away to brush tears from his cheek. 'I'm sorry,' he said. 'I told you I had enough to contend with. Day after day, the thing stares me in the face—and my poor mother keeps asking when my father is coming home. Well, my dear, I've said rather more than I meant to when I first came. You don't want to believe me, I can see that, but bear my words in mind. Jeffrey Maldon may be the only helper at hand, but that doesn't mean you have to grow fond of him into the bargain. Should he achieve a miracle and save your father, pay him off with a good round sum. But better yet, replace him with someone else, someone whose motives are not in doubt.'

'Name me one person who would accept the post,' she riposted in a tart tone.

'Uncle Pierce, of course.'

'But he refused.'

'But that was only at first. He's had time to think about it since, and I'm sure if you really tried to persuade him he'd agree. And Uncle Pierce, as we all know, is no fortune-hunter.'

The echoes of that conversation rang in her ears the rest of the day. A Jacobite? Could it be true that Jeffrey was a Jacobite? She tried to recall what he had said in political discussions with the other gentlemen at dinner, but could remember nothing. It seemed to her that she had never heard Jeffrey voice an opinion on the Hanoverians or the government. Was that in itself suspicious? Most men were only too eager to hold forth about politics.

But no! She mustn't allow herself to be led into this kind of scared distrust. It had happened before and she had been proved totally and utterly at fault. She wouldn't wrong Jeffrey again by listening to his detractors.

Nevertheless she was very glad to hear the rattle of the carriage wheels next day, and see Gylo cantering ahead of the vehicle on the long drive up to the door of the Manor House. She couldn't prevent herself running out to greet the travellers.

Jeffrey swung down from the saddle to take her outstretched hand. He was about to say something, but at sight of the welcome on Amy's face he checked. For one extraordinary moment she thought he was about to fling his arms wide to invite her embrace. They stood, as if poised on the verge of some leap across the invisible gulf that always kept them apart, and it seemed to her that they spoke to each other—without words, without gestures, but from heart to heart, in a language more powerful than spoken phrases.

At that moment some understanding hovered on the edge of Amy's mind. She almost knew something of vast importance—but what? And about whom? Herself? Was there some secret about her own character that she could not decipher? Was there some part of her own behaviour that she did not understand?

If there had been no interruption, she might have run to Jeffrey and by contact with him might have understood the enigma. But the carriage was rolling up to the door, and the moment passed. When Jeffrey spoke, it was of something more urgent than her momentary bewilderment.

'Pray,' he said, 'don't be distressed if your mother expresses herself strongly. Her visit to the prison was more afflicting than she expected, because she was totally unprepared for the grimness of it.'

'Oh, poor Mama—is she very unhappy?'

'She has made herself quite ill, I fear. I wanted to forewarn you so that you wouldn't think it was anything serious with regard to her health.'

The carriage rolled up. Bryce jumped

down and opened the door. Without waiting for the steps to be let down Mrs. Tyrrell flung herself out, being caught by Jeffrey's strong arms and her daughter's lesser ones.

'Oh, daughter, that is a dreadful place!' she wept. 'It is not fit for a genteel female to visit.' And with almost hysterical animosity towards Jeffrey: 'You should not have made me go! It was very wrong of you!'

'Mama!' cried Amy. 'It was you yourself—'

At a shake of the head from Jeffrey she broke off. 'Come, Mrs. Tyrrell,' he said, 'you had best go to bed. Amy, see her upstairs. She needs to be comforted and looked after.'

'Ye-es,' she agreed unwillingly. 'But you will wait? I want to hear your news.'

'Of course.'

She assisted her mother up the staircase and with Molly's help got her to bed. For nearly an hour she was busy, but at last hurried downstairs. 'Sir!' she cried, her voice shaking with a variety of emotions at being at last alone with him. 'How indebted I am to you for taking care of

Mama! And you are not to be hurt by her words to you.'

'Of course not. She was overset. She had no idea, of course, what a prison would be like.'

'Did it affect Papa very much?'

He gave a half smile and a little shrug. 'I fancy your father is accustomed to your mother's reactions,' he remarked. 'I was somewhat brief with her afterwards, I fear, which has added to her sense of injury.' He paused. 'But I had a great deal else to think of.'

She drew him to sit beside her on the settee opposite the fire. 'What has happened? Something is wrong?'

'Not exactly wrong, but we are now caught in a trap of urgency. I regret to say the trial is fixed for the end of this month.'

'So soon?' she gasped.

'I must tell you frankly that the quickness of the event is due to the Pegmen's machinations. They want it over and done with as soon as possible—it is to their advantage.'

'Oh, Jeffrey—shall you have the defence ready by then?'

'Not unless I can find at least Stephen Boles—and that brings me to the next point, the news I have had concerning him. David Bartholomew sought me out in Winchester—'

'Bartholomew—the riding officer for the Customs Department? What was he doing in Winchester?'

'He had been at Ringwood in the New Forest, mingling with the smugglers. The Pegmen have been gathering from as far away as Kent. They wouldn't come so far for nothing. It seems as if they intend to try something at Poole, where their contraband cargo is locked up. And yet,' Jeffrey said, rubbing his chin, 'I can't believe they will be so mad, with a naval vessel at the ready in the harbour. Ah well, that's neither here nor there for the moment.'

'No, sir, you were speaking of Stephen Boles.'

'Yes, Little Stephen, as I hear he is called among his friends. The rumour in the alehouses is that Little Stephen is to go to France soon.'

'To France?'

'So the talk goes. There is to be some

234

great stroke by the Pegmen, after which they will have a great deal of money, and Little Stephen is being sent to France to invest some of it in new cargoes of brandy and silk.'

'To France?' she said again, clutching at the sleeve of his riding coat. 'But we cannot let him go abroad!'

'How can we prevent him? We don't even know where he is.'

Amy tried to sort out her busy thoughts. 'Perhaps it is no bad thing if he is not present at the trial,' she suggested. 'His evidence was wholly against my father, so it is perhaps best that he is not there to give it.'

Her hand was still on Jeffrey's sleeve. She felt him sigh. 'If only that were true,' he murmured. 'But his evidence *will* be given.'

'How can that be, if he is not there?'

'Don't forget that he gave it on oath at the inquest. On the basis of that evidence the jury brought in a verdict of murder against your father, and on that verdict he was charged. The testimony given by Little Stephen is in the court record—it is admissible evidence. And ...'

he hesitated, but decided to go on, 'if he is not there, the evidence cannot be challenged by cross-examination. Your father's counsel would have to do the best he could to counteract its effect without being able to put a single question to that lying rogue.'

She bowed her head in dismay at the words, but in acceptance of his judgement of the situation. 'Oh, Jeffrey,' she whispered. 'What can an advocate do in the face of such circumstances?'

'Little enough, I fear. Yet he must do his best. I am writing today to an acquaintance in London who may be willing to go into court with the case.'

'Is he a good pleader? Will he be listened to?'

'He'll do his best, I have no doubt—but to be plain with you, Amy, his skill as a pleader is not the main point. We have to find someone with courage enough to take the case.'

'And this man has?'

'I believe so. He wasn't afraid to defend some of the Jacobite lords after the insurrection.'

Just as she had been able to feel his

sighing by means of the contact of her hand on his arm, so now he felt her stiffen. He glanced down at her.

'What's the matter?'

'He defended Jacobites?'

'Indeed he did, very ably—though without success, since the case against them was lost from the outset.'

'What do you mean, lost from the outset? You are not saying the Crown was determined to condemn the defendants if they were innocent?'

'They were condemned because they were Jacobites. Whether they had given active support to the rebels seemed scarcely to matter.'

'I'm surprised, sir, to hear you speak as if you think they were harshly treated. At least they were given a trial. One cannot be sure that the Stuarts would have given a fair trial to their opponents if they had won their fight.'

'Ah, come now,' he said in a tone of reproach, 'that is mere prejudice speaking. There were good and noble gentlemen among the Jacobites.'

'My father never thought so, sir!'

'And it is of your father we should be

speaking, ma'am, not of some political disaster of the past. To return to the point—'

'Are you a Jacobite, Mr. Maldon?'

The sudden return to formality of address alerted him to the fact that she was very perturbed. He sighed inwardly. 'Who has been speaking to you of Jacobites?' he inquired. 'Why are you so quick to pick up that subject?'

'You have not answered my question, sir! Are you a Jacobite supporter?'

'No, Miss Tyrrell, I am not,' he said with cool precision. 'And now that you have my answer, do you believe it? It isn't likely I would admit my political beliefs to you if I *were* a supporter of the Stuarts, in view of your hostility to them. So what have you gained by challenging me?'

'Are you saying that you would lie to me, sir?'

'I am not saying either one thing or another, Miss Tyrrell. I am trying to find out what you think should be done next for your father—who is languishing in Winchester Gaol while you waste time getting in a miff over imaginary Jacobites.'

'Sir, you are impolite!'

'Madam, you are absurd! Are we discussing Mr. Tyrrell's defence or are we having a quarrel?'

She jumped to her feet, her hazel eyes blazing. 'Don't speak to me as if I were a baby, sir!' she cried. 'You are the most impertinent man I have ever come across!'

'More impertinent than Bernard Gramont, who apparently reduced you to tears yesterday when he called?'

'Ah, so you know of that? Cross-questioning my servants?'

'Of course not. Palmer told me of it when he brought me some food, out of a wish to be helpful. He said I might find you a little upset because Mr. Bernard had been here "lowering your spirits"— but, faith, I find your spirits high and fiery, not lowered!'

She had actually been on the verge of sweeping out of the room in indignation, but she heard the amusment in his voice. She paused and turned back. 'Are you laughing at me, sir? '

He rose, came to her, and took her by the shoulders. 'Amy, you are a source of continual wonder to me,' he confessed. 'I never know from one moment to the next how you are going to react! When I arrived you were all eagerness and cordiality—now you are ready to box my ears, are you not?'

That had been true—a moment ago. Now she gazed into his ice-grey eyes and found laughter there. Her own wrath began to dissolve. 'Oh, lud, let us not get in a pet with each other,' she said on a note between exasperation and amusement. 'Matters are much too serious for that. Tell me, sir, what are my father's chances at the trial?'

'Poor, I'm afraid. We must prevent the trial taking place, as I told you at the outset. But I certainly didn't think it would prove so impossible to find witnesses who had seen Beau Gramont alive and well after your father left Parall that night. Little Stephen was my chief hope, but he is very elusive.'

'Stay!' she cried. 'Nancy seemed to know where he might be found!'

'Nancy?'

'Nancy Saythe—at the dressmaker's house. She was on the verge of telling me something when … when … well, the long and the short of it is, I never heard the end of the sentence.'

'Is she still there? At Miss Hilderoth's?'

'I believe so, Jeffrey. Why?'

'Because, if she has a *tendresse* for this man, she may be eager to keep him in this country. If I go to her and explain that Stephen Boles is about to quit the country but can be detained as a material witness if she will tell me where to lay hands on him, she may tell me.'

'You are right!' she exclaimed. 'The last thing Nancy would wish to hear is that Stephen is off to France! Oh, Jeffrey, it's worth trying!'

'Then I will go tomorrow and speak to her.'

'Why not today? Why waste time?'

'Because I have to write to London and get the letter away today. Moreover, I don't believe Miss Hilderoth would let me past the door. I need to find out how to get at Nancy Saythe by some backstairs method. But don't be afraid, Amy, I shan't delay over this matter.'

'Of course, sir; forgive me for interfering. You know best.'

To her surprise he took both her hands in his and held her away for a moment as if studying her. 'That is a phrase I never expected to hear from you,' he said with a laugh. 'Are you saying that you trust me?'

'Why, I—certainly I trust you—that is, I—'

'Nay, admit it, you were in great doubt only a moment ago whether I was a scoundrel.'

'No, that's not true!' To her own surprise, she pulled him close by the hands he was holding and stood staring up at him, as if she could read his very soul by the deep gaze. He did not flinch, but looked back at her.

A strange warmth seemed to run through her veins as they stood thus, face to face. To her dismay, it was she who turned away. She found she was trembling —but with what emotion she could not tell.

'I must not delay you, sir,' she said, in a voice she wished was less shaken.

She had the feeling that he had gently touched the nape of her neck. With his fingertips? With his lips? When she dared to look up, he was gone.

CHAPTER 10

Mrs. Tyrrell felt better the following morning but decided to stay in bed to recover from her travelling. This meant that Amy had to sit and read to her from *Clelia,* although she would much rather have been downstairs on the watch for Jeffrey Maldon.

By mid-afternoon there was still no sign of him. When at last a caller came, it was someone who appeared at the back door with his cap in his hand and a note for Miss Tyrrell.

'Robin Emhurst is here, miss—son of Farmer Emhurst.'

'To see me?'

'Yes, miss, a message from Mr. Maldon.'

Without waiting to listen to her mother's protests she threw down *Clelia* and ran downstairs. The lad was standing in the middle of the room, clutching a folded paper. When she unfolded it she found a few lines in Jeffrey's broad, firm hand.

'Nancy Saythe was extremely perturbed by my news of Stephen's likely departure, but it was a mistake to say I could detain him as a witness—she was alarmed by that and refused to give me any information. I had the feeling she intended to get in touch with Boles, so I have kept watch thus far, with Robin's help. She has now walked out on the Poole road with a bundle over her arm which appears to contain her belongings. I am following in hopes she is going to find Boles herself. You shall have word as soon as possible.'

Amy looked up. 'You have spoken to Mr. Maldon, Robin?'

'Yes'm. I was in Markledon today bringing in eggs for the market. He asked if I'd help him and of course I said yes at once.'

'So what did you do?'

'I took some eggs to the back door of Miss Hilderoth's shop, pretending they'd been ordered. Then I got a chance to speak to Nancy and told her someone had news of Little Stephen for her, at the Garland.'

'I see. So that's how Mr. Maldon got a chance to speak to her.'

'Yes'm. But she were only there a minute or two. She came scurrying out with her face all scarlet and a-clasping her hands. I saw her speak to Timothy Bentworth, that was a friend of Little Stephen's—but he shook his head and she ran back to Miss Hilderoth's. So me and Mr. Maldon, we watched the shop, him at the front and me at the back, and after one o'clock dinner she come out and went off on the high road. Mr. Maldon rode after her on Gylo but came back after a few minutes to write this note for you, miss.'

'Thank you for bringing it, Robin. And so Mr. Maldon has ridden off after Nancy again?'

'No, miss, he hasn't gone a-horseback. That black o' his, it's a sight too notice-able. Nobody in the district has a better beast. He's gone on foot, 'cos Nancy's on foot after all.'

'Towards Poole?'

'Aye, and if it's Poole she's heading for—as I daresay it is—that's nigh twelve mile, a long enough walk in this mizzly weather and with the wind rising. Perhaps she'll get on the stage wagon—today's a day for the stage wagon, Mondays and Thursdays ...'

Amy had had experience of waiting for parcels to be delivered by this cumbersome conveyance, that took goods and passengers cheaply, though slowly, from village to village.

But that meant that it might be twenty-four hours, or even forty-eight, before she learned whether Jeffrey had been led by the servant girl to Stephen Boles.

'Thank you, Robin,' she said. 'Now you must have something for your trouble.'

'Nay, Miss Tyrrell, Mr. Maldon give me a sixpence, though I'd have done it for nothing for your sake, miss.' Blushing and embarrassed, he bowed himself out.

Amy's mother couldn't imagine what ailed her for the rest of the day, she was so restless and nervy. 'Really, daughter, one would think it was you who had her sensibilities affronted by the gaol at Winchester instead of me,' she complained.

'I'm sorry, Mama. But I don't feel like

reading to you anymore.'

'Very well, sit down and let us play bezique—that will keep you occupied enough, I hope!'

Since it was useless to look for news that day, Amy resigned herself to the role of nurse and companion. But the following day her mother was up and about again, and Amy's time wasn't occupied in amusing her. She kept watch by the window in the breakfast room, but no one came up the drive.

Arguing with herself as the hours went by, she tried to put forward all the events that might delay him. He might have lost track of Nancy. He might have been turned away by Stephen Boles. He might have been set upon—he might be hurt!

At this she began to pace up and down the breakfast room, clasping and unclasping her hands. The suspense of not knowing what was happening was unbearable. In the end her good sense came to her aid: she must do something herself, or she would go out of her mind.

She had already had the passing thought that it might be worth while paying a visit to Uncle Pierce. First of all,

Bernard had hinted that the old man was repenting his cowardice; he might now be willing to help Jeffrey prepare her father's defence and, certainly, if the case was going to come to trial as now seemed likely, it would be a benefit to have a respected local lawyer involved in the defence. The judge would be impressed by that, even if the jury—who would mostly be smugglers or their supporters—were not.

And then there was the question to which she herself would rather like an answer: what was the information about Mr. Maldon that Uncle Pierce had had from his London friend?

Her mother was vexed when she appeared dressed for the ride to Markledon. 'You are not going out, Amy?'

'Yes, ma'am, I am going to see Uncle Pierce.'

'But you know I am not well.'

'Mama, you are much better than yesterday, and besides, I am not good company today.'

'Well, that is true, at any rate. Very well, my dear. But pray hurry back. Evening is coming on—it will be dark soon after six.'

'Yes, Mama, I promise to be back soon, and if darkness has come on Uncle Pierce will send Datchett to accompany me home.'

Her mother was quite satisfied with that. Amy hurried out and rode away before Mrs. Tyrrell could delay her any further.

When she turned into the little lane off the High Street she thought she saw Uncle Pierce's servant in conversation with another man, in front of the door of the house. Nothing unusual in that—except that she was almost sure the man was Timothy Bentworth.

Tim Bentworth had been the foreman of the jury at the inquest, foreman of the jury that had trapped her father into a murder charge. It was accepted—by Jeffrey Maldon and Farmer Emhurst and everyone else who viewed the event dispassionately—that that jury had been made up of Pegmen or men with the fear of death put into them by Pegmen.

Yesterday, when Nancy Saythe hurried away from the Garland Inn, she had stopped to speak to someone—so Robin

249

Emhurst had reported. To whom had she spoken? To Timothy Bentworth, 'that was a friend of Little Stephen's', as Robin Emhurst said.

And now here was Timothy Bentworth in conversation with Datchett, Uncle Pierce's manservant. That was worrying. It meant that even in this household, there might be spies at work. She must mention it to Uncle Pierce.

The two men parted company as Watched trotted up to the door. Datchett stood on the doorstep, looking quite unwelcoming. 'Did you want to see Mr. Pierce, miss?'

'Of course, Datchett.' Why else would she be here?

'He's very busy today, miss.'

'But not too busy to see me, Datchett.' After all, she was his god-daughter.

'Please to wait, miss. I'll go and inquire.'

She sat down in the hall, feeling distinctly unwanted. It was perhaps the first time in her life that she had ever been kept waiting in Edward Pierce's house. Outside the wind racketed round the eaves as a harbinger of one of the autumn storms that so often pounded upon this coast. The seas would be running high tonight; even from the Manor House, which was a mile or more inland, they would be able to hear the pounding of the waves on the cliffs at Hengisbury and Bower as the wind carried that mighty sound.

The long-case clock in the hall ticked loudly. From within Uncle Pierce's office she could hear the sound of voices. Once she thought she heard laughter and the clink of glasses, but the old oak door was thick and made a good barrier against eavesdropping.

Perhaps it was true that she had come at an inopportune time. All the same, surely Uncle Pierce could leave his cronies for five minutes to speak to her? She had a sudden sense of isolation, as if no one in the world wanted her. It was the last thing she ever thought to experience in this house, where she had run in and out as a child with Bernard.

At length, after a wait that began to seem almost uncivil, Datchett appeared. 'Mr. Pierce can spare you a few moments now,' he said, and ushered her into the office.

Uncle Pierce rose momentarily from behind his desk but did not come forward to greet or kiss her. He was a little flushed, as gentleman often became—so Amy had noted—when they had taken drink.

'Forgive me for keeping you in the hall,' he began, waving her to a chair. 'I had friends with me that I couldn't get rid of very easily.'

'It is I who should apologise, Uncle Pierce. Perhaps my coming here is an embarrassment—'

'Nay, nay, it's just that we had a little something to celebrate and I didn't want to cut it short.'

'I'm happy to hear that. Is it something I may know of?'

'Oh, a good stroke of business, that's all,' he replied, waving a hand in airy dismissal. 'And now, my dear, what was it that brought you here?'

'Something that I dare say could have waited till another time, Uncle. However, since I am here, perhaps you may know that Bernard has paid me a visit?'

'Did he indeed? He murmured something to me of intending to put matters right between you. I hope he did so.'

'Well, as to that,' she said, unfastening her cloak and letting the hood fall back to be more comfortable in the stuffy room, 'he made an explanation of his presence at Miss Hilderoth's, which I accepted though I don't necessarily believe it.'

'Dear me!' Uncle Pierce pushed his silver-rimmed spectacles up his nose and peered at her through them. 'I never thought to hear you speak of Bernard in quite so cool a tone, Amy.'

She sighed. 'I have learned a great deal in these last few weeks. I remember how vexed I used to be with Mama because I thought she was a romantic, but it seems to me now that I was as romantic about Bernard as she was about his father. But it's useless to regret all that now.'

'Good, good. I'm glad to hear you take it so well. So now all is calm between you and Bernard? Thank you for letting me know.' The old man's hand was hovering over the bell on his desk, as if he were about to ring for Datchett to show her out.

'Oh, but that isn't the reason for my

visit,' she said in haste. 'I came to ask if, as Bernard suggested, you would be willing to resume your role as my father's lawyer?'

'Resume my role?' Mr. Pierce said, staring at her in amazement.

She was a little startled at the surprise he was showing. 'I'm ... I'm sorry,' she faltered. 'Have I embarrassed you? Bernard said you would be willing to ... and ... well ... I thought if I came to put the idea to you ...'

'Hey-day! A very cool tone indeed! I had never imagined so much icy realism in your nature, Amy.'

His response puzzled her even more. He seemed to be speaking almost entirely at random. But then, she reminded herself, he had been drinking. The taint of spirits was still quite strong in the room. She decided not to try to make sense of the strange remarks about icy realism and go on with her plea.

'Papa would be pleased,' she pointed out. 'I think it has hurt him very much that you did not come to his help at first—oh, I don't mean to reproach you. I quite understand that you were made nervous by the atmosphere of menace that surrounded us. But Bernard said—'

'It was very wrong of me,' her uncle agreed with a little tilt of his head. His expression was strange, almost amused. 'I am prepared to make amends now by doing all I can, but you mustn't imagine that I am able to career about the country like your young knight errant—'

'Of course not, sir, that would be inappropriate and unnecessary.' After all, she told herself, Jeffrey could still take the lead in all the activity; Uncle Pierce would be most useful in offering experience, and knowledge of local dignitaries. 'So it is settled, then? You will help to prepare my father's defence?'

'I'll do what I can, Amy. As soon as the countryside has settled down a little I'll go to Winchester to see him.'

'Thank you.' She paused. 'I think, though, that the countryside is as settled as it is likely to be for a long time—'

'Nonsense! This recent attack has set the whole population in a flutter.'

'What attack is that, Uncle Pierce? I don't quite understand you.'

'You haven't heard?' His bushy grey

eyebrows went up. 'Then I don't quite see—' He broke off to study her for a moment or two. 'Your request to me for help seemed to imply that you had been given the news, but then—perhaps you didn't connect one event with the other.'

'What event, sir? You are talking in riddles!'

'You haven't heard the second item, obviously. The Custom House at Poole has been broken open and the Pegmen have got all their confiscated goods back. They are now marching at leisure back to their homes, with various bundles of contraband. That is what I meant when I said the countryside was unsettled.'

Amy was aghast. 'They dared to do that?' she cried. 'It actually happened? Jeffrey said they never would dare.'

'Jeffrey has been proved wrong, in this as in other matters,' he replied with a glint of satisfaction.

'But the naval sloop? How could they dare attack the Custom House with naval guns directed upon them?'

'Because, my dear Amy, they chose their time with great good sense. At about nine o'clock this morning, the tide was full out, leaving Poole basin a sea of mud. The sloop was stuck in it like a wasp in honey. Her guns could not be brought to bear on the shore.'

She shook her head in dismay at the picture he conjured up. 'How dreadful!' she gasped. 'And yet ... We ought to have foreseen this ...' She let her mind run over the conversations she had had with Jeffrey on this matter. 'It was perplexing that the Pegmen seemed to be gathering for a stroke of some kind even though the *Nymph* was on patrol. Now, of course, everything is explained. They had realised they were safe at low tide.' She threw up her hands in annoyance. 'Oh, one would have thought the captain would realise that, too!'

'Perhaps he did. But you know, my love, these rascals have friends everywhere, even in the Navy. Doubtless some clumsy mariner mishandled the steering or the mooring when there was full water in the harbour, so that just enough tilt was given to the decks to make the guns point skywards ...' Uncle Pierce chuckled. 'Forgive me, my dear, but it has a comic side!'

'Not to the men who risked their lives to capture that contraband cargo from the smugglers,' she countered. 'And the dragoons—what are they doing as the Pegmen march across country?'

'Well-a-day, there's another disaster! They're on quite the wrong side of the district. By the time they've been marched from Milford, the contrabandists will be safe away with their belongings.'

'Their belongings! You speak as if they had some right to those goods, whereas the tea and brandy and lace were brought into the country illegally—had been confiscated by the crew of the *Swift*. Oh, how Papa will be vexed when he hears of it!'

Uncle Pierce was still chuckling a little. ' 'Pon my soul, Amy, if your father had been less busy in vexing himself over such things, he wouldn't be where he is to-day!'

'You see something amusing in it?' she exclaimed.

'Forgive me, my dear.' He recovered his gravity. 'But after all, who is hurt if the free-traders bring in a cargo or two? Why need he have been so strong against them?'

'Who is hurt? Why, Uncle Pierce, you have had this discussion with him many times and agreed with his conclusions. We are all hurt, are we not? The whole countryside is kept in a state of fear so that these men can bring in their shipments.'

'Nonsense! No one need be in fear. All that's needed is a little discernment about where it's safe to go and what it's safe to see.'

'You yourself have said it—safety! We are none of us safe while these men flout the laws.'

'The laws against the importation of tea and spirits are stupid—'

'If they are stupid, then they should be changed,' Amy said with warmth. 'And if they are to be changed, they should be dealt with in Parliament—not by terrorising farmers and cottagers or bribing officials. Parliament is the place to argue out this problem, as my father has always maintained.'

'Faith, you are as foolish as he is, child,' her uncle said in a terse manner. 'I've no patience with you.'

'You cannot be serious in exonerating the Pegmen? You cannot condone their marching about the district after breaking open one of his Majesty's warehouses?'

'Let us not discuss it. We shall only disagree.'

'Ye-es,' she said after a momentary pause. 'I am surprised to find that you say something quite different to me now from what you used to say to Papa.'

'Ah well—your papa is out of the way now, is he not?'

All at once she looked at him with the keenest attention. His cheeks flushed with drink, his eyes glittering with satisfaction, the amusement he had shown when describing the humiliation of the naval contingent, the views he had just been expressing with considerable conviction ...

'That was what you were celebrating,' she murmured. 'The stroke of good business that had pleased you was the freeing of the contraband from the Custom House!'

'Now, now, let us forget the whole thing.'

'You had money invested in that cargo—is that it? And now instead of a loss you will make a profit?'

'Amy, let us not speak of it. I'm sorry if I allowed my sense of humour to get the better of me. I'm an old man, you know. I must be allowed some eccentricities—'

'Of course!' she went on, disregarding him. 'Now I understand why Timothy Bentworth was here when I arrived. He had just brought you the news of the attack at Poole.'

'My dear, you are leaping to conclusions—'

'No, no! A hundred little things begin to come together!' Her voice rose as utter conviction began to take hold of her. 'Beau Gramont, by his own admission, was involved in the smuggling trade, but Jeffrey always said he didn't have enough brains to direct the work.'

'It's unfair to accuse Gramont,' Pierce broke in. 'He is dead and can't defend himself against the charge.'

'Faith, he admitted the charge!'

'To whom, child? What nonsense is this?'

'He told my father on the night of the quarrel—in fact, that was what the quarrel was about.'

'Ah,' said Pierce, sitting back in his chair with an air of regret. 'Too bad. I hoped he would say nothing about that, seeing that Bernard warned him how it would grieve you if Bernard were arrested too.'

'It was his intention to say nothing,' Amy replied, 'but Jeffrey Maldon persuaded him to speak.'

'Truly, that gentleman has been quite a thorn in our flesh. It would have been far better if your father had gone to his death with that secret still preserved.'

'Better?' she gasped. 'Better if Papa died?'

'Now, Amy, I didn't mean it like that,' her godfather reproved, 'you know I did not. I never wanted to harm George. I am not a man of violence—'

'Oh no,' she interrupted in scorn. 'You leave the violence to others! In this case, you would have let the law get rid of the man who has taken action to prevent your smuggling activities.'

'You are angry about it,' he said, nodding, 'and it isn't to be wondered at. But consider how long I protected him! For a dozen years and more all went well. I

262

was able to get forewarning of any scheme he was planning—'

'Yes, through spies in his own home!'

'Well, was that not better than having to have him killed? Ah, many times that course was urged on me, but I refused, Amy—after all, he was my friend—'

'Your friend?' she cried. 'Have you any idea of the meaning of the word? Have you any conception of right and wrong?'

'I know what is right for me, child— that's what's important. I haven't survived in this harsh world for more than sixty-nine years without learning how to pursue my own advantage. And all might have gone well for years to come, if only that fool Gramont could have resisted his clever little joke about the *Swift*. I saw suspicion dawn in your father's face that night when he heard Gramont's words. Can you imagine how I felt at that moment, Amy? After all the years of keeping the simpleton safe from his own obtuse acts of virtue, I knew I should be forced to silence him.'

'What did you plan to do?' she inquired in a hard voice. 'Kill him?'

'I had to consider it. But then the

necessity was removed when Stephen Boles came running to see me soon after midnight with the news that Gramont had babbled to your papa, and that Boles had made sure Gramont would never be arrested and questioned by government men by simply putting an end to him there and then. Almost at that very moment I saw how it could be turned to our advantage.'

'By making sure the jury at the inquest was primed to bring in a verdict of murder against Papa—an inquest conducted by you, the man he had trusted his business affairs to for twenty years!'

'Spare me your reproaches, child. I did what I had to do.'

'I don't understand your reasoning,' she replied in a tone of horror. 'In what way were you forced to trap him?'

'I have a network of workers depending on me, Amy. I could not let George endanger all that I had built up. If he had talked—and been believed—I might have suffered a great financial loss.'

'You will suffer more than that! The penalty for smuggling is hanging.'

'Oh, I shan't suffer, my dear,' he said

with tolerance. 'I never allow events to fall out so that I suffer.'

'I think you will find that you are about to enter on a different era,' she said, getting up. 'Your days of supremacy are over.'

'Nonsense. I intend to go on as before, for many years.'

'Not when I tell what I have just learned.'

'Really? To whom shall you tell it? What proof shall you present?'

'I shall report everything you have said, word for word—'

'And I shall deny it.'

'Then we'll see which of us will be believed! I can gather proof—'

'My dear Amy, you'll do nothing. Now that you're alone, the world will understand that grief and anxiety have affected your reason.'

'Oh, you mean that I will be classed with poor Mrs. Gramont? Out of my senses?' She tossed her head as she moved towards the door. 'You forget I have a helper who will know that I am quite sane, and who will know how to handle the knowledge that you have just given me.'

'Are you speaking of Bernard?' Pierce interrupted. '*He* will do nothing to help you. He is only waiting for the day when your father will be safely hanged!'

She was shocked into standing still. 'Bernard? Bernard is in this with you? I don't believe you!'

'I see you have still some fondness for him—'

'Why not? We have been friends—' She broke off. 'But I have just been learning how little friendship means. Yes, and now I think of it, Bernard has acted as your messenger, has he not? Running to me with your slurs and aspersions on Mr. Maldon—trying to drive us apart so that I should be friendless! It's true, I once asked the question myself—why should Bernard dislike Mr. Maldon so ...'

'Bernard is a great baby,' Pierce said impatiently. 'His one concern is to look after his mother, who really is in a very bad way, poor soul. Now that his father is gone he turns to me for advice and guidance.'

'And he will take over the role that Beau Gramont used to fill?' she demanded, thinking with dismay that Bernard's spendthrift ways would make him an easy target for Pierce's machinations.

'By no means. Beau was always a nuisance—I only put up with him and his womanising because we needed the cellars at Parall to hide our goods. That was why he came here, you know. I could see great possibilities in the grounds at Parall, but it would have been quite unsuitable for a country lawyer like myself to buy such a house. So I brought Beau to the district—and then when, like every new owner, he began having "improvements" made to the grounds, no one thought it strange. No, no, Bernard has inherited the house, but that is all he has inherited. He never took any part in our activities except to help spend the profits. I think the best plan will be to offer him a good price for the house and then move someone else in.'

'I am thankful to hear it,' she said. 'Even now, I shouldn't feel happy to bring trouble upon Bernard.'

'Oh, my child, do please stop talking nonsense! You are not in a position to bring trouble upon anyone. You may cause a little stir at first with your accusations, but people in authority soon become weary of ladies with tales of woe to tell.'

'But they will listen to Mr. Maldon.'

The old man stared at her from faded blue eyes. 'Mr. Maldon?'

'Yes, and pray don't trouble to make your usual claims that he is a fortune-hunter or a trouble-maker. I understand now that from the first you needed to turn me against him so that he would be dismissed from the case, thus making my father's death almost certain. But you've failed there, as you'll fail in any scheme to cast doubt on him when he acts on what I'm going to tell him. He'll put you in the dock, Mr. Pierce!'

'I don't think so, Amy,' he responded in a strange tone.

'You'll see!' she cried, full of confidence. 'With what you have told me, he'll find some means of—'

'No, he won't, my love.'

'But he *will!* He is clever and quick—cleverer even than you, Mr. Pierce!'

'His cleverness will avail you nothing, my poor child. He will never do anything for you again.'

Her breath caught in her throat. Suddenly the stuffy room seemed like a tomb, the panelled walls were closing in like the sides of a coffin.

'What do you mean?' she gasped.

He took a moment to reply. 'Faith, we've been at cross purposes from the beginning,' he muttered. 'Do you think I'd have talked so freely to you if that young Galahad of yours was likely to hear of it? But mind you, I *was* a little surprised by the coolness with which you accepted the situation.'

'Situation? What situation?'

'Naturally when you asked me to take over your father's affairs again, I thought you knew that our good Mr. Maldon had left the scene.'

'But where has he gone?' she blurted out, childish in her bewilderment.

'Where, indeed?' Pierce pointed with a wrinkled finger. 'Above or below? Who can tell? It all depends whether he has led a good life, does it not? But perhaps you could influence the direction of his journey, my love, if you believe in the power of prayer. I think there's still time for a few well-directed pleas to the Almighty on his behalf.'

'What?' she cried, her senses whirling. 'Speak plain, Uncle Pierce! Don't play games with me—not on this! Where is Jeffrey? What has happened to him?'

The old man got up from his chair and came to her. 'Sit down, child. Why, you've gone as white as a sheet.'

'Don't touch me!' She sprang away from his outstretched arm. 'Don't touch me, you evil, wicked man! What have you done to Jeffrey?'

'I? I have done nothing, Amy. I told you—I am not a man of violence. But he has caused a great deal of annoyance to my friends, and when they saw an opportunity of getting rid of him it was too great a temptation. Tim Bentworth was just reporting that to me as you arrived.'

Amy's mind could scarcely take in what he was saying. 'You—were laughing!' she faltered. 'I heard you—while I was sitting in the hall!'

'Aye, well, to me it is a matter of amusement, you see, my dear. It's such an inglorious end for one so tall and imposing! Rather like Swift's Gulliver, you know—roped up on the beach—'

'No!' Amy screamed. 'No, you *could* not—you *could* not!'

'But I'm afraid they have, Amy. You know it's their favourite way of making an example of their enemies. And Maldon has been an enemy to us—oh yes, troublesome and clever. This scheme of his to follow Nancy Saythe to Poole so that he could find Little Stephen—'twas a famous notion. But nothing Mr. Maldon did escaped our observation, Amy. We had learned that he was to be reckoned with. And so Tim tells me they knocked him on the head outside the Clasped Hands and brought him back with them as they marched away from Poole until they found a suitable spot on the beach—'

'Jeffrey!' Amy cried. 'No, no—I don't believe it!'

'Go and look for yourself, then, child. You'll find him stretched out for the tide to drown, if it hasn't already done so.'

All at once an icy calm descended on Amy. She turned once more to the door. When she reached it she paused. 'If you have harmed him,' she said, 'if he is dead … I swear to you that I will never rest until you have paid for it. If it takes me the rest of my life, you shall dangle at the end of a rope for the murder of the man I love.'

Even the self-satisfaction of Edward Pierce was not proof against the fierce coldness of her words and the glitter of her hazel eyes.

'Nay, Amy,' he protested, 'I—I didn't know you cared for him in that way.'

'Nor did I,' she said, 'nor did I. But if he is dead, something in me has died also—that part that would make me shrink from watching you pay for your crime, Edward Pierce.'

Next moment she was outside, the self-control already beginning to crumble into a ruin of despair and grief.

'Jeffrey,' she whispered, 'Jeffrey—oh, my love, where are you?'

Somewhere on the long stretch of shore that ran between Markledon and Poole, the man she loved was bound hand and foot to strong pegs driven into the sand, waiting for the seas to wash over him with the finality of his death sheet.

She stood for a moment, listening. She could hear the waves rolling in, rolling in.

CHAPTER 11

As she galloped out of Markledon, her one thought was to get to the beach. Watcher's hooves struck sparks from the cobbles on the bridge as she crossed the river, heading out of the High Street towards first the pack-road and then the heathland that stretched away to the ironstone quarries on the higher ground.

The quickest way down was at Hengistbury, where an easy slope had seen the drag-and-tackle of many a smuggling party bringing contraband ashore. But Hengistbury was east of Markledon, whereas the attack party from Poole had come from the west. Amy's brain, beginning to function as she rode into the boisterous wind, told her that the smugglers would not have gone further along the shore than they need, loaded as they were with bags of tea and casks of brandy. They would have strapped Jeffrey down at some point along their route. Somewhere between Markledon and Poole—but that was a long stretch of shore, about twelve miles, and included the jutting sandbanks along the front of Poole Harbour known as the North Haven.

She judged that the Pegmen would have gone across Poole Heath to Bourne Bottom, which was the easiest route for laden men and animal. They would have taken the road up Penny's Hill and then struck out to the south-east to the path along the cliffs when they reached the Bourne. The cliff road would be safer for them in case the dragoons caught up with them, for then they would only have to defend themselves on one front while the cliffs and sea would make their other bulwark.

So somewhere between Bourne Bottom and here, they must have taken Jeffrey down on the beach to tie him down. The first essential was to get down on to the sand.

She beat Watcher unmercifully to make him stretch out at his fastest pace. They went plunging down the sand dunes at the creek south of Carbery, the gorse catching cruelly at their sides. Watcher snorted and shied, frightened at what she was asking. Ahead of him in the gathering gloom was a stretch of grey water, rolling in in white-edged heights that roared and crashed only a few yards off. He had never been on the beach before, and the damp, yielding sand underfoot alarmed him, the approaching and receding of the sea was unnerving, while the cliff that began to grow tall above him as he galloped cast a shadow from the right.

The shores of Hampshire and Dorset are different from the rest of Britain. Everywhere else has two tides a day, but here, because of the race of water caused from two directions by the Isle of Wight, the tide comes in twice in twelve hours.

Amy was no fisher-girl, but she had been born and bred in these parts and already her mind was working out the tide times. Pierce had said the Pegmen attacked the Custom House when the harbour was a sea of mud; she recalled that he had fixed the time as "about nine o'clock". So at about noon, the sea would have been up to the quay at Poole, and it would be up to the cliffs here at that time also.

It was due to reach the cliffs again about six o'clock. As she had fled from Markledon she heard the church clock strike six, so there was not a moment to lose. One thing was in her favour—the wind that had been rising all day. It was an off-shore wind, delaying the tide by perhaps as much as ten or fifteen minutes by the mere force of the air beating against the incoming waves.

'Faster, Watcher, faster!' she sobbed, leaning forward along the back of the frightened pony.

He scrambled on, hooves sinking into the sand, flanks beginning to heave from fatigue in these unaccustomed conditions. Now there were boulders and rocks among the sand and he reared and flung himself sideways as his eye caught a great shape that could have been a monster but was only a weed-covered stone.

Amy threw herself from his back and, holding him by the reins, picked her way among the rocks. Only a few feet away on her left the sea made sucking sounds amongst them. There was but a narrow corridor now between the sea on one hand and the cliffs on the other. Watcher pulled back, anxious to be out of this trap. But she dragged him on, and a few minutes later was rewarded with easier going, smoother sand.

And there, a hundred yards ahead, she caught a gleam of fair hair on the ground. She called, but the sound of the cry was lost in the roar of the surf and the moaning of the wind.

'Jeffrey! Jeffrey!' She let go of Watcher's rein and ran forward. Yes, now she could make out the shape stretched out on the beach. The long body lay with the arms pulled up and stretched outwards, the dull blue of his riding coat against the wavering beige of the sand.

'Jeffrey! My darling!' She ran. The wind caught at her cloak, whipping it back from her shoulders. She let it fly away behind her, exposing her cheeks and neck to the cold spray. She heard a flurry of sound but didn't turn as Watcher, terrified at the great bat-like flying thing, turned and raced away.

She threw herself down on her knees at Jeffrey's side. The scatter and sprawl of her arrival in the sand made him turn his head as far as he could, and she saw in the waning light the astonishment in his clear grey eyes.

'Amy! What in God's name are you doing here?'

'Oh, thank God, thank God! You're alive! He was wrong—the tide hasn't claimed you yet. Wait, Jeffrey, you'll be free in an instant. Wait till I untie the ropes. Oh, Jeffrey!'

Sobbing and laughing, blinded by her own tears, she scrambled up the slight slope of the beach to his right hand, which was wound about with inch-thick rope attached to a stout stave hammered into the ground. She clawed at the bond, but it was iron-hard, tied by an expert and made all the more immovable by the dampness that had seeped into it from the sand.

Her nails broke, the skin tore off her fingers. The knot remained unchanged. She felt the sea rush over her feet and the hem of her riding skirt.

'I can't!' she panted. 'I can't! Oh, God, I can't untie it!'

'Amy—'

'There isn't time,' she sobbed, 'we have only a moment or two. There's something I must tell you, Jeffrey—I want you to know—'

'Amy, listen to me—'

'No, no, let me speak!' she cried. 'I won't leave you—you won't be alone, Jeffrey. I shall die with you, because—'

'Don't be a fool, Amy!'

The words were like a whiplash. They cut across the hysterical avowal of love she'd been about to make. They actually stung her physically so that she threw up her hand to her cheeks and sat back, gasping in pain.

'We're not going to die,' he said, raising his voice so that it could be heard above the roar of the breakers. 'If you'll catch hold of your senses we can be out of here in minutes.'

'Oh, if you think I'd go without you—'

'I said "we", not "you", though by heaven I'd rather die by myself than let you sit there weeping by my side.'

'Oh!' she gasped. 'But I—but you—'

'Be silent and do as I tell you. Amy—there's a knife in my pocket.'

'It's useless, useless ... What?'

'A knife, you madwoman! A *knife!*'

'A knife?'

'In my pocket. Get it out!'

'Which pocket?' she cried, suddenly coming to her senses under that crisp command.

'Damn it, I don't know—but stop crying and *find it!*'

She thrust her raw and bleeding fingers into the capacious pocket of his riding coat. She felt the usual paraphernalia that men find it necessary to carry—a kerchief, a pencil, a pocket notebook, coins, a little box for flint and steel and then ... yes ... the cool and solid shape of the folded pocket knife.

'I've got it,' she cried. 'Wait, I'll open it!'

Easier said than done. She had torn away her nails so that she had nothing to put into the little niche that would pull out the hinged blade. She delved in his pocket and found a small coin. Using that, she prised the knife blade out.

To cut a rope with a knife sounds a simple undertaking. But this was a small knife, intended for cutting quill pens or perhaps leather harness throngs; whereas the rope was thick and strong. She sawed at it, weeping again in panic and frustration, telling Jeffrey that the strands were parting although not a shred seemed to be cut.

'Push the point into the hemp, Amy—don't try to cut right through, dig pieces out. That's it, that's my brave girl. Again.'

He was speaking to her as if she were a child. She resented it with one half of her mind, yet it steadied her. She dug at the rope, and a piece came away.

'Good. Now the other side of the fibres.'

The blade slipped. The point went into his wrist. 'Oh, heaven!' she cried. 'Oh, forgive me, Jeffrey!'

'Never mind, never mind. Oh, don't start whimpering again! Amy, stick to the matter in hand.'

'Whimpering?' she repeated. She bit her lip. 'I'm *not* whimpering!'

She began to saw savagely at the hempen strands. All at once she was business-like and steady. She felt the sea rush up the sands to the place where she was kneeling. When it receded it only went as far as her feet. She was drenched and cold. For Jeffrey it was even worse—his long body was stretched out into the rising tide, the edge of his coat was beginning to float this way and that with the waves. The light was fading fast now.

Bending close to his wrist, she dug and cut the rope. Now the strands were beginning to spring apart. 'Pull, Jeffrey—can you pull against it?'

She saw his fist clench as he heaved against the bond that held him. A third, fourth and yet a fifth strand gave way. She worked at the remaining twist of hemp, not daring to look round at the sea which she could feel at her knees.

And at last, under the combined efforts of her knife and his tugging, the last of that fetter gave way. His right hand was free.

'Give me the knife,' he commanded.

She obeyed. He turned on his left shoulder and with his right hand began to cut at the bond holding the left hand.

'Go now,' he said, without turning back to her.

'Go?'

'Climb the cliff. The tide's coming

in fast.'

'But I can't go without you!'

'Do as you're told! Climb the cliff!'

'No!' she wailed, tears returning. 'I won't go without you.'

He turned his head to speak to her sternly, and as he did so his numbed hand lost its grasp of the knife. It slithered down his arm and disappeared under the shallow water that had now crept almost to his chest.

'Confound it!' he swore, 'it's gone!'

'I'll get it.' She leapt up and ran round to his other side, where she began to ferret about beneath the little waves.

'Don't do that!' he exclaimed. 'You'll bury it in the sand.'

'But I—'

'Sit still a moment. Now … it must be somewhere close to my shoulder. Feel about gently.'

'Yes, here it is. I've got it now. Let me do it, Jeffrey. Your hands have lost the sense of feeling.'

'Give it to me, Amy. I command you, give it to me—and get off this beach on to the cliff before you are stranded.'

'I don't go until you go.'

He gave up the argument. 'All right, fetch me a stone to sharpen this blade.'

'A stone?' she echoed blankly. 'What use is a stone?'

'To get an edge on the knife, of course. Oh, don't argue at every word, girl— fetch me a flat stone!'

She scrambled up and felt about in the gloom. She felt a pebble about six inches across, with a flat surface. She held it out to Jeffrey who, with ten or twelve strokes of the blade across it, whetted the edge to a razor sharpness.

After that it was the work of a moment to cut through the rope at his left wrist. 'I should have sharpened it days ago.' he panted as he sat up and set to work on the ties at his ankles, invisible under the water. 'It only goes to show that we shouldn't put off till tomorrow what we can do—'

'How can you quote proverbs?' she cried. 'Quick, quick, the tide's flowing in fast.'

'I'm coming.' He staggered up, swaying a little. 'God, I'm numb all over.'

'Lean on me.'

'Quick, Amy, we must get up the cliff.'

Instead of placing his hand on her shoulder for aid, he gave her a sharp push towards the headland. 'Move, girl, move!'

She tried to obey, but her heavy riding skirt was sodden. It tangled itself around her limbs so that she couldn't stride forward, but instead fell face down into about twelve inches of sea water. A wave surged over her. She screamed in terror and the sea rushed into her mouth. She felt herself choking and flailed about with her arms.

Someone caught one flailing arm and dragged her upright. Someone said encouragingly in her ear, 'Come, don't drown yourself like a kitten. Up, up— on to the cliff.'

'I can't,' she gasped, 'I can't—'

'You *must.*' He put both arms round her from behind and lifted her forward. The heavy skirts untangled themselves in the water and she was able to walk. Half walking, half being lifted, she made the few yards to the foot of the bluff. The water was at knee level, surging strongly among the boulders at the foot of the sandstone face. Jeffrey let go for a moment and stared up.

The sky was dark grey now. A young moon was beginning to spread a little light among racing clouds. The wind had turned, as it is wont to do after sunset, so that now it was helping to drive the tide in.

'Do you know this place? Is there a path?'

'I ... I don't think so.'

'Further along? If we edged along the foot of the cliff?'

'I don't think so. The nearest is Bourne Bottom—we might be in water over our heads by the time we reached—'

'Very well, we must take our chance here. Quick, on to this boulder, Amy—'

With his help she managed to get on top of it. From there she would have to step on to the almost perpendicular wall of sandstone. There was a narrow ledge, made perhaps by rabbits who had burrows on the heathland above. She nerved herself to make the step, but could not.

'Quick, Amy, quick!'

'I can't!'

'In God's name, why not?'

'I shan't be able to keep my balance.

My clothes are weighing me down like a net of stones.'

He climbed on to the boulder and stepped across on the narrow ledge, a little above her. He held on with one hand to a tussock, reaching out with the other. 'Come, Amy.'

She moved her feet. The serge skirt dragged like a fetter. 'I can't, Jeffrey, truly I can't. My skirt is so full of water.'

'Then take it off.'

'What?'

'If you can't climb in your skirt you must climb in your petticoats.'

'Sir, how dare you!'

'Oh, don't be missish about it, girl! Which would you prefer—to be dead and decent or alive and immodest? Untie the skirt and let's be up out of this tide water!'

Thankful that the darkness hid her scarlet cheeks, Amy untied the tapes that drew together the top of the skirt under the little tight-waisted jacket, and let the full flounces slip down over her hips. The skirt fell round her ankles on the rock. The waves were already licking there, moving the heavy brown serge this way and that like some great piece of seaweed.

Clinging against her legs now was what had once been an elegant underskirt of fine cambric and ruched lace. It was most improper to expose it to view, but it *was* much less heavy than the discarded skirt.

'I'll go up and pull you after me. Are you ready for the first step?'

'Yes.'

'Very well—come now.' He held out his hand again and this time she stepped forward on to the ledge.

Her foot found a precarious hold. She was standing beside him, very close. He put his arm about her to steady her.

She was shivering with cold and fright. Her hair had gone into little damp ringlets that had the tang of salt. He could hear her breathing, fast and ragged. He wanted to tell her that she was the bravest and finest girl in all the world, but knew that one gentle word would unleash floods of tears.

'I'm going up the next foothold. Stand very still.'

'Yes.'

'When I stretch down my hand to you, come at once.'

'Yes.'

His long legs took him upwards to a better spot, a little rounded outcrop of rocks where a pool left by the last tide had not evaporated. He knelt in it and leaned down to drag her up again. She clambered towards him, tearing the fine fabric of the underskirt, but no longer caring about that as she heard the waves foaming just behind her.

Up they went, yard by painful yard. It seemed a thousand miles to them, although it was only a little over a hundred feet, but every move was dangerous, footholds were few, and the cliff crumbled dangerously under their combined weight on the resting-places.

The very last few feet were the worst, for the rock had an overhang and he was almost too exhausted for the physical feat of grasping it, swinging himself out from below and then got up. The rock-edge broke away in his hand. Earth and broken turf fell on Amy's head and shoulders. She cried out in terror.

'Jeffrey! *Jeffrey!*'

Silence. And then, as she began to huddle against the cliff in despair, she saw a long arm come down.

'I'm here, I'm here. Catch hold. Now, don't be afraid, Amy—you'll dangled in mid-air for a moment but you'll be safe, I swear to you. Just hold on, that's all.'

'Yes … yes.'

She put her hand in his. She felt his fingers close over hers. If I fall, she thought, I'll be dashed to pieces on the rocks below or drowned in the sea … Goodbye, Jeffrey, my love, my darling …

'Are you ready? No nonsense, now—hold on like the devil!'

Jolted into awareness, she grasped his one hand with both of hers.

'Now,' he said, and heaved her upwards.

She felt her feet fly outwards, felt herself suspended like a fly in a spider's web. Then she was being dragged on to the short turf, face-downwards. She could smell the salty tang of sea-pinks and purslane. She dug her hands into the yielding earth. She was safe.

After a moment she felt herself being pulled up into a sitting position. 'Amy, are you all right? Did I hurt you? Say something—tell me if anything hurts?'

She leaned against Jeffrey's chest. She could hear his heart pounding. His arms were around her. She huddled close, shivering.

She felt very small and frightened in his arms. He wanted—more than he had ever wanted anything in his life—to put his mouth on hers and by doing so give and take reassurance that they were still alive. In the fitful light of the cloud-skimmed moon he could see a pale, tear-stained face, eyes huge with emotion, one little battered hand pushing back the wet hair from her cheeks.

'Oh, Amy,' he whispered, capturing her hand and holding it gently. 'Poor little girl …'

She made a little sound. Perhaps it was pain from the cuts on her fingers. Perhaps it was weariness. It cut through all his defences, and he pulled her against him to comfort her.

For Amy it was paradise to have him hold her close. Death had been so near that to be alive was a miracle—but to be alive and in Jeffrey's embrace was an unbearable bliss. For a moment consciousness almost seemed to slip from her.

She lay against him, her head on his shoulder, her arms winding themselves about him.

Which of them set lips upon lips, it was impossible to say. But the kiss swept them away more strongly than ever the tide could have done, to a land of glory and wonder. Amy was afraid to breathe, afraid it was some wild delirium that had seized her in reaction to the danger she had undergone, afraid it would fade if she so much as let her heart beat. She wanted to pour out her feelings, to tell him that she loved him—but she dared not, for fear of wrecking the dream.

For his part, Jeffrey had lost control of his emotions to an extent he would have thought impossible. He felt her arms around his neck, he felt the tangle of curls against his cheek, and he drank in the intoxication of the kiss to the full. But in a moment he sensed her utter stillness. Misinterpreting it, he struggled to make himself release her. She had only wanted comfort ... Well, he would not add to her ordeal by offering more than that.

She could not guess what it cost him to draw away from her. He looked at her.

She was trembling—perhaps with cold, perhaps with shock. She watched him uncertainly, wondering why he rejected her.

'Up,' he said briskly. 'We mustn't sit here gaping at each other or we'll die of the cold.'

'Oh,' she said in a groan of despair. 'I can't ...'

'I mean it, Amy. The cold of this wind could kill us both. Come on, up with you.' He got up and dragged her with him. He took off his heavy riding coat and draped it round her. 'We must get you home.'

'Home? But it's miles—'

'Where else are we to go? Not, I think, to Markledon!'

That brought back to her mind the scene she had left in Markledon. 'Jeffrey, I thought you were dead!' she wailed.

'I very nearly was. And I nearly died of fright when you appeared. I thought you were an apparition!'

'Don't joke, Jeffrey. Mr. Pierce boasted that they had killed you.'

'But he surely didn't tell you where to find me?'

'Only that he had left you to die in the traditional Pegman fashion. It had to be between Markledon and Bourne Bottom, or at least so I thought. Thank heaven I was right!'

'Amen to that.' He paused as he urged her into movement. 'I haven't thanked you yet for saving my life.'

'Oh ... As to that, I think you saved mine also.'

'But you wouldn't have been in danger if you hadn't come to find me.'

'Ye-es ...' She rubbed the remains of tears from her cheeks, and didn't look at him. 'I made an awful fool of myself, though—becoming as panicky as a school-girl ...'

'I was a little panicky myself,' he said.

'But you didn't let it show. I feel I behaved like an idiot.'

'We shall both look idiots if, having saved ourselves from the incoming tide, we die here of the cold and the ague—so come along, let's get ourselves moving.'

With an arm about her, he made her walk along the path at the top of the cliff. The gorse tore at their clothes and dragged at their weary limbs. The wind beat against them. The darkness itself was an enemy, for they could not see where they were putting their feet. Amy's little riding boots of thin red morocco were soon cut to shreds by the stones. Their progress became painfully slow.

Jeffrey was alarmed. He was serious about the result of the wind's cold on their exhausted bodies. He had heard of men who had died simply from exposure. He urged Amy forward, and when she began to make little weak protests he scolded her.

'Are you a weakling, then? What will your father say if he hears you gave up? Come, Amy, show what you're made of ...' But he could feel that he himself was losing the remains of his strength under the need to support Amy more firmly.

As the outline of the rounded barrows at Hengistbury showed against the flying clouds, a shape suddenly started up in front of them. Amy gave a shriek of fear, but Jeffrey lunged forward after it. He had heard a well-known sound—the clatter of hooves on the stony path.

'There, there, poor boy,' he soothed, moving towards the white shape in the gloom. 'What a state you're in.' His hand touched the neck of the horse. It trembled but stood still. He felt along until he could gather up the reins. Then he led the beast back to Amy.

'Why, it's Watcher!' she cried. 'You wicked boy—you ran away!'

'Well for him,' Jeffrey said with reproof. 'We had little chance of saving *him*. He must have galloped back and got on to the land at Hengistbury. Now, let me help you up and get you settled ...'

She felt she ought to say that he should ride also, but by now her mind was too full of cotton-wool to make sense of her thoughts. Jeffrey was better able to judge that the nervy little pony, all covered in dried sweat and sand, would never take the two of them. He led the horse, trying not to let the weariness of his hand drag down the poor beast's head.

Amy found that, now she no longer had to make the painful effort of walking, fatigue threatened to engulf her. The light swaying step of the pony became almost a lullaby. She felt herself sagging forward, starting awake as she almost lost her balance. Her hands were too chilled to feel the bridle.

All at once there was a light shining in her face. Voices were exclaiming. She pulled herself erect on Watcher's back.

They were at the Manor House. The front door was open. Palmer was there with a lantern, holding it high while he stared in consternation. Molly, her maid, was having hysterics behind her apron.

As Amy blinked at them stupidly, her mother came hurrying out on to the front steps.

'Mr. Maldon!' she cried, throwing up her hands. 'What have you done to my daughter? Sir, you will pay for this!'

Amy slithered down from Watcher's back, throwing out a hand towards her mother in protest. 'No, no, Mama—'

'Please to go, sir!' her mother ordered. 'And never come back here again!'

The last thing Amy saw before a fluster of hands and voices claimed her was Jeffrey Maldon's back as he set off down the drive on foot, with her mother's reproaches following him like nightbirds' calls.

CHAPTER 12

When Jeffrey awoke next morning in David Bartholomew's house, he found the Preventive officer already up.

'Faith, so you've come back to life, Mr. Maldon!' he cried. 'You've been sleeping like the dead, and the story all round the alehouses last night was that you'd been done away with!'

'Yes, near enough, I confess,' Maldon said, yawning and stretching stiff muscles. 'David, where are you off to?'

'Well, to tell truth, sir, I've just come in. I've been out all night looking for you, or what might be left of you.'

'Thank'ee, but someone else succeeded in that role yesterday', Jeffrey said with a wry smile. 'If you're free to undertake it, David, there's work for you. You must go in search of the dragoon officer and have troops sent to Parall.'

'To Parall?'

'Yes. While I was in the hands of the Pegmen yesterday they were very free-spoken. I learnt that they were on their way to stow their goods in a cellar at Parall.'

'Are you sure, sir? I've never seen smugglers going in and out of the house.'

'No, and for good reason. The cellar is under the ornamental lake.'

'Under the lake?'

'Exactly. When Beau Gramont bought the house it was quite natural for him to have improvements carried out to the house and grounds—and one of those improvements was to have a huge cavern hollowed out with an entrance in the spineey at t'other side of Parall's grounds from Mr. Tyrrell's house. They were able to carry the goods under the boundary fence and into the cellar without ever being seen.'

'It was Mr. Gramont, then ... the man who laid out the money to buy the cargoes?'

'No, the venturer was—and still is—Edward Pierce. A clever old fox. I'll thank you to tell the dragoons to put a watch on his house until the warrant can

299

be sworn out against him.'

'And young Mr. Gramont, sir?' Bartholomew inquired, taking notes. 'Shall I have a watch set on him?'

He saw the other man hesitate. The fair brows drew together. 'Not for the present,' he said. 'I have no grounds for suspecting him of anything.'

'Oh, come, Mr. Maldon. Are you saying he didn't help his father?'

'I don't know. It may be that Beau Gramont didn't trust his son enough to let him take part in the business.'

'Aye, that's possible. A foolish enough young man, Mr. Bernard Gramont. But is there anyone else the soldiers should be on the lookout for?'

'Stephen Boles, who was with the party attacking the Custom House at Poole yesterday,' Jeffrey said. 'But I fear you won't get him. He was due to start for France as soon as the contraband was taken out of the warehouse.' He sat down wearily on the rough wooden chair near the fire. 'I wish we could take him. It was he who killed Beau Gramont.'

'Truly, sir?'

'Yes, he boasted of it to me yesterday.'

Jeffrey shrugged. 'He thought, of course, that I wouldn't live to tell the tale. And although he was wrong, I think he'll elude us. That doesn't matter, however. My sworn deposition ought to be enough to have the inquest verdict set aside.'

The riding officer, who had taken his instruction so far without demur, glanced at him now from shrewd black eyes. 'So you have enough authority for that?'

'I believe so, David. Besides, I can identify at least half of that inquest jury now as being active smugglers. Their verdict against a magistrate is bound to be biased, and the charge against Mr. Tyrrell that they brought in could not be allowed to stand. But better yet, I have actually heard the real culprit admit to the act—and so Mr. Tyrrell must be set free. If you will take a letter, which I'll now write, to the captain of the militia, he will see that it reaches Mr. Pitt in London— and from there I believed it will only be a matter of hours before an order is signed for the release of Mr. Tyrrell.'

The sturdy little riding officer threw himself on Jeffrey. 'God bless you, sir! You've done what I almost believed impossible! Well, let me shake your hand! I'm your friend for life, sir—believe me, for life!'

When he had written his letters and sent off the Customs man, Jeffrey washed and changed in preparation for a task yet to be accomplished. Little though he relished the thought, he must speak to Bernard Gramont. Amy had a fondness for the man, perhaps still hoped to marry him. That being so, Jeffrey must give him what chance he could to take himself out of the way of trouble.

As he was preparing to set out, Amy Tyrrell was waking up at the Manor House. She felt bruised and stiff. Her hands were smarting where the salt water had penetrated the cuts and grazes of yesterday. But nevertheless she was well, with that additional sense of well-being that comes from a great danger success-fully overcome.

Molly set to work upon her hands with unguents and lotions and strips of court plaster. Then she had breakfast while the maid did what she could with her tangled hair. After a long session with hairbrushes and hairpins, Amy felt she looked at least presentable. She put on a gown of apricot dimity, to reflect some colour into her pale cheeks. Then she felt ready to face the world.

To her amazement, her mother was already up and about when she came downstairs.

'Well, miss?' said Mrs. Tyrrell. 'What have you to say for yourself?'

'What, Mama?' Amy replied. It wasn't the kind of question she had expected. She'd thought her mother would make tender inquiries about her health.

'I never saw anything so disgraceful,' Mrs. Tyrrell surged on, scarcely waiting for an answer. 'I suppose you know that your reputation is quite gone?'

'My ... reputation? But, Mama—'

'I thought it dubious when you came back from Winchester with him, though perhaps it didn't matter too much because no one actually saw you. But last night— in *Markledon*—everyone who knows us must have seen you in that disreputable attire!'

'Mama,' Amy said, beginning to grow angry, 'I was not in Markledon in my underskirt, if that is what is worrying you.

I was on the beach near Bourne Bottom.'

'On the beach? On the beach? In your underskirt? Daughter, don't dare to say such a thing to me—'

'And I took off my riding skirt because I had to climb a cliff.'

'A cliff?' Mrs. Tyrrell sat down on the nearest chair. 'You climbed a cliff? To get away from him?'

'From whom? From Jeffrey? You must have taken leave of your senses, ma'am! If Jeffrey hadn't helped me up Bourne Bluff, I should be washing about in the sea off the chines by now.'

'Daughter, you will please not take that tone with me. It is most undutiful! From now on I intend to take a much firmer line with you instead of letting you ride about the country and visit Winchester—'

'If I am undutiful, I apologise, but I will not have you speaking as if I had done something reprehensible, particularly as that casts a slur on Mr. Maldon too.'

'Don't speak of that man to me!' her mother cried. 'Bringing you home in that shocking condition!'

'I hope you didn't address him with the kind of nonsense you have just been speaking to me, ma'am.'

'I spoke to him as he deserved. I ordered him from the door and told him not to come back.'

'You did what?' Amy said faintly.

'Warned him off! He'll not be back, I warrant you! Even a fortune-hunter as brazen as he—willing to wreck a girl's reputation so that she has to marry him—even *he* wouldn't dare to come back after being forbidden the house'

'Mama!' Amy said. 'You did not say anything like that to Jeffrey?'

'I didn't waste words—no, not I,' Mrs. Tyrrell replied with satisfaction. In her own mind, the scene of last night had been transformed a little. The reproaches she'd cast at Jeffrey Maldon were now, in her memory, full of dignity and scorn instead of the cries of shock they had been in reality.

She stared now as her daughter hurried to the door. 'Where are you going?' she cried.

'To find Jeffrey—to apologise!'

'You'll do no such thing! Sit down, miss!'

'I'm sorry, ma'am, but I must disobey

you. I *must* speak to Jeffrey.'

'You are to stay where you are,' her mother cried. 'I insist. You would not actually flout my direct command?'

'Yes, Mama, I'm afraid I would,' Amy said. She paused and came back. 'Dearest Mama, you are under the greatest possible misapprehension! Jeffrey has done nothing to harm me or my reputation, I assure you. Have I ever lied to you? Have I ever deceived you?'

'We-ell ... no ...'

'Then believe me when I tell you that last night Jeffrey and I were in great danger of drowning under Bourne Bluff. Between us we managed to scramble up the cliff face, but I could never have done it without his help. He then brought me home, although he was so weary he could hardly put one foot in front of the other—and now I learn that you turned him from the door!' Amy's voice broke. 'Oh, how could you, ma'am! The best friend, the most honourable friend ...'

'Oh, now, daughter,' Mrs. Tyrrell said, beginning to be perturbed by her daughter's vehemence. Could she have done the wrong thing after all? 'You know you always thought he was a fortune-hunter—'

'No, I did not! I had some such foolish notion for a time, but I soon learnt my error. He has endangered his life for us— we owe him more than we can ever repay!'

'But you can't expect me to think well of a man who leads my daughter into scrapes such as last night,' said Mrs. Tyrrell, pulling at the lace side frills of her cap. 'And he took me into that dreadful prison—'

'But only because you insisted on going, Mama. And then,' Amy said with a sigh of distress, 'you broke down and made an exhibition of yourself, just as I did yesterday. He must think we are a parcel of fools.'

'Well, if he has a low opinion of us, it's as well if he doesn't come to the house!'

'*That* is mere foolishness. Even if we are fools, we must be grateful and polite fools, ma'am. God knows how we are ever to make amends to him for the insults we have heaped upon him. Oh, I have done my share of that,' Amy said, her voice breaking. 'You are not alone,

Mama, in misjudging him and speaking your opinion. But I must seek him out now and apologise—'

'No, no, Amy,' her mother interposed. 'Truly, child, you don't look well, and I beg you not to go rushing off in search of the man. Let Bryce be sent with a letter to him.'

'But that is so cold, so impersonal.'

'Write with warmth, then, if you must,' said Mrs. Tyrrell, giving up the fight. 'I confess I don't understand how you come to have so much emotion on the subject, but I can see you are in earnest. Tell him I apologise, tell him to come and see you, tell him ... tell him I regret what I said last night. I may have been too severe. But let me tell you this, daughter,' Mrs. Tyrrell ended, 'if matters go on as they are, you won't have a shred of reputation left!'

Since she could see her mother was determined not to let her go in person, Amy sat down to write a note to Jeffrey. It proved extremely difficult. It was all very well for her mother to say: Write with warmth. But how much warmth? Last evening, when she had come upon

Jeffrey tied down on the sands, she had been on the verge of telling him that she loved him. But before she could get the words out, he had told her not to be a fool!

From that point, it was hard to find a path between her real feelings and the need to hide her secret. She wanted to write, 'Please, please come and see me—I am dying with longing to see you—until you come I feel my heart will beat with only half its strength.' Instead she wrote, 'I learn that my mother received a wrong impression from our arrival last night and want you to know that she withdraws her prohibition ...'

She scratched out and re-wrote for half an hour. In the end, she gave up and began pacing about, lost in thought, remembering the events of last night.

She recalled all she had learned, about Mr. Pierce and the death of Beau Gramont and the smuggling and ... And Bernard? Was Bernard involved?

Once she told what she knew, Bernard *would* be involved. She must speak to Bernard. She hurried out, pausing only to pick up an Indian shawl as protection against the October breeze.

She went through the wicket-gate and across the lane into Parall's grounds. As she did so she heard the sound of a horse coming at a neat trot and, turning her head, saw Jeffrey on his big black coming sedately up the drive.

'Jeffrey!' she cried in delight, and ran to meet him.

'Good morning, Amy,' he said, swinging down and doffing his hat. 'How are you this morning?'

'Well enough, thank you. And you?'

He had taken her hand. He looked at the little thimbles of court plaster that Molly had put over each broken nail. 'Poor little fingers,' he said in a gentle voice.

'And you?' she said, looking at the weals on his wrists. 'Have you put any soothing ointment on?'

'Nay, all that will take care of itself,' he said. 'And is your mama still in a fury with me for bringing you home in your petticoats?'

Amy blushed and turned away.

'I fear we shocked her, Amy.'

'I fear so. But she might have waited

before ... Ah, well, it's useless to expect Mama to change now. She has always been inclined to speak before she thinks.'

'I wish she liked me better. I don't exactly know what I have done to set her against me so ...'

Amy couldn't explain it either. It was just one of her mother's incomprehensible views, likely to be changed as suddenly as it was adopted.

'And are you just about to visit Bernard, or are you coming from there?' he went on.

'I'm just going there.'

'And so am I. Shall we go together?'

'Why are you going there?' she inquired, her mind beginning to work. 'Did you learn a great deal yesterday, before those dreadful men tried to kill you?'

'A great deal, Amy. And you too, I gather—because you said last night that Pierce boasted he had killed me.'

'Yes. I went to see him ... because of something Bernard had said to me. And somehow he ... I don't know ... little by little it all came out. I think he had had too much to drink, and was flushed with triumph over the attack at Poole. And he thought it didn't matter to tell *me,* because no one would believe me.'

'But *I* shall be believed, Amy.'

'Indeed?' She looked up at him, puzzled and yet trustful. 'I of course would believe whatever you tell me. But I wonder if it will prove as easy to convince the gentlemen of this county, who have known Mr. Pierce all his life?'

'Never fear, Amy. I shall be believed and your father will be set free.'

'You mean it?' she gasped. 'He can be restored to us?'

'I promise you. And you too, Amy— you can have your life restored to you. Your life, and the man you love.'

She stared at him, perplexed.

'I can free Bernard too,' he went. 'Bernard is—'

'Oh, you mean that you can somehow protect Bernard from any charge of being a confederate of the Pegmen?'

'Not only that, my dear. Bernard has been in the greatest distress since his father died, for a reason that has divided him from you with more force than you can imagine. I am now going to explain to him that he has been duped, and once he knows that there will no longer be a barrier between you.'

They had been walking on slowly as they talked, with Gylo stalking disdainfully behind them. They now reached the door of Parall, and it flew open to reveal Bernard. He had clearly been watching their approach from the window.

He stood in the doorway staring at them. 'What are you doing here?' he said to Jeffrey. 'I thought I told you never to come to my house again?'

'Calm yourself,' Jeffrey said. 'I've come on an errand of mercy—'

'How could you bring him here, Amy? You know how he has been persecuting us!'

'I know nothing of the kind, Bernard. Jeffrey says he wants to help you and I believe him.'

'You believe him? He is making a fool of you.'

'Come, Gramont,' Jeffrey said, 'let us go inside—or do you prefer that we discuss your mother's illness on the doorstep?'

Amy saw Bernard go pale and lick his lips. 'You dare to come here with some charge to make against my mother?'

'Why should you jump to such a conclusion? It's quite groundless.'

'Let's go indoors, Bernard.' Amy, at a nod from Jeffrey, led the way. The drawing-room still had the shutters closed, although it was now mid-morning. The place had a forlorn, un-lived-in look.

'Please say what you have to say and then go,' Bernard said. 'I don't want you here causing trouble.'

'I've come to do just the opposite, to clear away the misery and suspicions that have been making you ill ever since your father's death—the secret that has weigh-ed so heavily on you, that has prevented you from offering any help or kindness to Amy, that has prompted you to wish to see Mr. Tyrrell hang—'

'Jeffrey!' Amy cried in horror. 'Pray don't! Mr. Pierce said some such thing to me, but I cannot bear it—'

'It's true nevertheless,' Jeffrey insisted. 'But you'll pity him when you hear the reason. He thinks his mother killed his father.'

A moment's stricken silence followed.

'No, no, it's not true,' Bernard burst out. 'She didn't do it! It was Mr. Tyrrell—'

'It was not!' Amy cried. 'How could you think such a thing?'

'He doesn't think so, Amy. Truly he doesn't. But he has to act as if he does, otherwise you might have suspected what he *believed.*' Jeffrey went to the other man and quite gently pushed him into an elbow chair. 'Gramont, you rushed to a conclusion that seemed possible, perhaps even probable. But you should have been wary of Edward Pierce!'

'Mr. Pierce? How does he come into it?' Amy cried.

'It was to Pierce's advantage to let Bernard think his mother was guilty. That way, Bernard would work hard at getting someone else condemned. You couldn't expect Bernard to want to see his mother in the dock.'

'Oh, no,' Bernard groaned, hiding his face in his hands. 'Oh, no, it would be too dreadful.'

'And so Bernard did all he was asked by Mr. Pierce. He tried to get me pushed out of the way. He wanted your father

315

to be condemned—'

'An innocent man?' Amy cried.

'At least you knew your father was innocent. Bernard knew—or thought he knew—that his mother was guilty.'

'No, no—'

'Don't bother to cry out about it, Bernard. The agony is over. You may have found her with the dagger in her hand when you came running at her screams, but all she had done was *pick it up*. She found your father dead in the hall when she came downstairs, as I imagine she often did, in search of him. Loving him as she did, she made an outcry—did she not?'

'Why ... yes ... yes ... you seem to know a great deal?'

'I heard it described when I was held prisoner by the Pegmen yesterday. Stephen Boles thought it very comical that he had killed Beau Gramont but got two other people condemned for it—Amy's father by the inquest jury, your mother by yourself.'

'Stephen Boles? Little Stephen?' Bernard gasped, a wild light of hope dawning in his eyes.

'The very man. Edward Pierce's hench-
man. After he had stabbed your father,
Boles hurried to Pierce to tell him what
he had done. Pierce came to Parall with
him, to find you trying to comfort your
mother, who was out of her mind with
grief. Was it then that he planted the idea
in your mind that your mother had committed the crime?'

'I ... I ... don't remember.'

'Well, she was perfectly innocent. She
was unable to explain that she had found
her husband dead, because she never got
her wits back. All this time you have been
protecting her—and it is understand-
able—but you have been quite in error.
What is worse, you have been aiding and
abetting Pierce to put Mr. Tyrrell's head
in the noose.'

'Oh, Bernard,' Amy said in a faint
voice.

'Forgive me—Amy, forgive me! I must
have been mad!' Bernard flung himself
out of his chair and knelt at her side.
'How I must have wounded you! I know
how you love me—I swear that I'll make
it up to you in the future—'

Amy snatched her hand from his

fervent clasp. Quite unexpectedly, she found she couldn't bear his touch. 'Control yourself,' she said in a strange tone, very cool yet shaken. 'I may have loved you once, Bernard, although it now seems strange and unlikely. But I have no wish to share any future with you.'

'Oh, I know you are hurt, and want to punish me.'

'I don't want to punish you. I wish you well, although it will make me very happy if I never see you again.'

'That is your pride speaking. I understand, truly I do.'

'Perhaps it is my pride speaking. But I think it is my common sense. I have wasted enough of my life on you, Bernard. I've other plans for the rest of it.'

'Other plans? But your father has always accepted that you and I are to marry—'

'I hardly think he will be eager for it when he hears the part you have played in his misfortunes. But putting that aside, he wouldn't wish me to marry a man I can't respect.'

'What?' Bernard gasped.

'Can't respect. It's too difficult to

explain, I fear. Let us merely say that if you feel any debt to me because of our childhood friendship or because of recent events, I absolve you from it.'

Jeffrey Maldon spoke for the first time in some moments. 'Are you sure you aren't acting out of momentary emotion, Amy?'

'I am sure. I have known for some time that I no longer care for Bernard.'

'But ... Amy ... what am I to do if you refuse me?' Bernard complained.

A dark sparkle came into Amy's hazel eyes. 'Well, there's always Miss Hilderoth.'

'Oh, so that's what this is about? But I explained about Miss Hilderoth.'

'Do you think you did? Well, never mind. I'm sorry, Bernard, with or without Miss Hilderoth, I could never marry you now.'

She felt that enough had been said and was turning to go. Jeffrey laid a hand on her arm. 'There is one thing more, however,' he remarked. He looked down at Bernard, who was still kneeling in a lover-like attitude on the floor. Flushing, Bernard scrambled up.

'Well?' he said uncertainly.

'Your mother is innocent. I am not so sure that you are. But I will give you the benefit of the doubt. In twenty-four hours a search will be made here and I have no doubt that large quantities of contraband will be found in the great cellar under the lake.'

'What?' Bernard exclaimed.

'You mean you didn't know about it? I wonder if a jury would believe that. I repeat, there are goods there that cannot be got rid of before the search party arrives—'

'How do you know this?' Bernard challenged. 'You speak of searches and juries and giving me the benefit of the doubt. Who are you to make accusations of this kind? You may be acting on Mr. Tyrrell's behalf, but that doesn't give you the right—'

'No, Mr. Tyrrell's case doesn't give me the right. But the duties conferred on me by Mr. Pitt give me authority to order searches and make inquiries—'

'Mr. Pitt?'

'The Paymaster-General. You must have heard of him.'

'Mr. Pitt?' Amy said, in wonder. 'Mr. Pitt sent you here?'

'Yes.'

'But why?' She shook her head in perplexity. 'I don't understand.'

'Mr. Pitt is charged with the task of raising money to pay the Army and the Navy and the Civil Service. Taxes which should provide the funds for them are simply not being paid. Worse, honest shopkeepers are being driven to bankruptcy because goods brought in at no tax are undercutting those on which customs duty has been paid. So Mr. Pitt sent me to Hampshire to try to find out, once and for all, how the smuggling rings work, who puts up the money for the cargoes, and how the cargoes are dispersed to the cities.'

'You are an envoy from Mr. Pitt?' Bernard said.

'An unacknowledged envoy. Naturally my mission had to be kept secret. If it had been known what I was here for, I should have been pegged out on the beach long before yesterday!' He smiled as Amy gasped, and went on with wry humour, 'I had not, as everyone seemed to assume, come to try for your fortune. I really am not a fortune-hunter, Amy.'

Amy felt herself going scarlet. 'I ... I never really thought you were, Jeffrey.'

'Oh yes you did, for a time. Particularly when Bernard put ideas into your head.'

Bernard moved restlessly about the room. 'I only passed on what I had been told—'

'By Edward Pierce.'

'Well ... yes ... But then, how could we know you came from the Paymaster-General? And indeed, I don't see why he should send you. Are you a particular protégé of his?'

'Not exactly. He needed someone for this particular task, and I had been brought to his attention over the Jacobite prosecutions.'

'Ah,' Amy said, with a glance at Bernard. Bernard looked away.

'Ah,' Jeffrey echoed mockingly. 'Was it Pierce who put the idea in your mind that I was a Stuart supporter?'

Amy sighed. 'Well, it was Bernard. Who had it from Mr. Pierce, I suppose.'

'Well, but,' Bernard broke in, 'it seems

there was truth in it after all!'

'Some truth. There were three poor Jacobite gentlemen in the Tower and, as far as one could see, no one bestirring himself to get their defence ready. And you know, a man is entitled to a defence, no matter how guilty he may prove to be in the end.'

'And so you came forward to help', Amy said softly.

'Yes. I made such inquiries as I could and persuaded a friend to plead their cause at the Bar—the same man who might have taken your father's case if it had proved necessary.'

'And what happened?'

'We failed, of course. But at least we tried.'

He was silent. Amy went to his side and took his hand. 'I honour you for what you did.'

'What, even though I was helping wicked Jacobites?'

She pressed his hand between both of hers. 'Jeffrey, she said. 'Oh, Jeffrey ...'

For a long moment their eyes met and held. The spell was broken by Bernard, who cried, 'Well, and how does Mr. Pitt come into that?'

'He had my name mentioned to him, sent for me, and told me he had a task that needed a man of some initiative. He put before me the idea of coming to the South Coast. I was quite unwilling at first. I don't see myself as a secret agent. But Mr. Pitt pointed out, with some truth, that after helping three Jacobite lords my career as a lawyer was likely to suffer a temporary check. And so, after some hesitation, I accepted his commission. And ...' he looked again at Amy, a look of sudden meaning ... 'I have never been sorry, despite the difficulties I've encountered.'

'Difficulties?' Amy cried. 'Oh, when I think what we have said and done to you!'

'Oh, come, you were not to know I was Mr. Pitt's employee.'

'And this is what you meant when you said that you would be believed concerning Mr. Pierce.'

'Yes indeed. I have already sent a report to London, and have asked for soldiers to help to round up the smugglers. Yesterday proved very informative, even though Nancy Saythe led me straight into an ambush at the Clasped Hands. From the statements that I can now make under oath and with evidence I hope to gain from some of the captured Pegmen—and we *shall* capture some—the withdrawal of the case against your father is certain.'

She gave him a sudden, unguarded smile. 'How wonderful you are,' she murmured.

'And are you to have me arrested?' Bernard cried. 'Is that what you are telling me?'

'Quite the contrary. I recommend you to take your mother and sisters and go, as quick and as far as you can.'

'Go? But ... but ...'

'You might ask Miss Hilderoth if she would like to go with you,' Amy put in, with impish good humour. 'To marry her here in Markledon might cause problems—but if you settled elsewhere no one would find it strange, because no one would know that you had once been the son of a landowner and she had been a dressmaker.'

'Leave Markledon?' Bernard said.

'Within twenty-four hours. The dragoons will be here soon.'

'But ... but ... What about Pierce?'

'What about him?'

'Are you giving him twenty-four hours' warning too?'

Jeffrey's mouth became a grim line. 'No, I am not. That gentleman has a great deal to answer for, not least the intention of seeing Amy's father at the end of a rope. Besides, it's already too late for him. I've got young Robin Emhurst watching his office and if he should make the slightest move to leave, I shall have him followed until the dragoons take him prisoner. But he won't bestir himself. He's too pleased with himself to imagine he can be arrested, and he still thinks my corpse is pegged on the beach, thus disposing of his one real enemy.'

Amy went close to him, shivering. 'It so nearly happened.'

'But for you, it would have happened. But you must forget such things, Amy. The future looks bright again, and everything will be as it used to be.'

'Not quite everything.' Amy went to Bernard and offered him her hand.

'Goodbye, Bernard. I don't believe we are likely to meet again. I wish you luck wherever you go and whoever you take with you.'

'Th-thank you, Amy,' Bernard stammered, taken aback by her calmness. 'I wish you happiness ...'

'Thank you.' With a slight curtsey she went out. Jeffrey joined her in the hall, offering his arm. To him she said, 'He may live a quiet and happy life after all—who knows?'

'His mother will be a worry to him for a long time, I fear. She loved her husband very dearly.'

'Oh, yes,' she idolised him. Poor Mrs. Gramont. And yet—'

'What?'

'A woman who has loved a man as deeply as she has is perhaps to be envied.'

'Perhaps,' he agreed. He opened the door for her and ushered her out into the October morning. The sun had overcome the chill breeze so that the walk towards the Manor House was very pleasant. Gylo could not be walked easily through the shrubbery beyond the wicket-gate, so his master tethered him there, to be taken round later to the stables.

'Now, I suppose, I must pay my respects to your mother,' he murmured.

'Yes, but she will suddenly learn to like you when you tell her that Papa is saved.'

'I hope so. I have a particular reason for wanting your mother's approval.'

'Indeed?'

'Indeed. But this is perhaps not the time to speak of it. We have been through a series of dramas and it would be unfair to ... to ...'

'Unfair?' Amy said, pausing and turning to study him. 'In what way?'

'Well ... I have a certain request to put forward, but ... I scarcely like to ... Although it reassured me to hear you tell Bernard so calmly that you had ceased to care for him some time ago.'

'Sir,' Amy said, tilting her head to look into his eyes, 'do you remember telling me once that when you had seen my father walk out of Winchester Gaol a free man you would present the bill for your services?'

He winced. 'Don't remind me of that conversation, Amy. I said things I didn't mean.'

'You didn't mean them? Now, there! How disappointing!'

'Disappointing?'

'As I recall it, sir, you took some slight payment in advance. I am interested to see what the full bill might be.'

'Amy!'

She saw the incredulity in his eyes, and gave a tremulous little laugh.

'In the fairy stories, you know, Jeffrey, the prince is asked to do half a dozen impossible things and then when he has done them he gets the hand of the princess. In this particular fairy story the princess was cross-grained and ungrateful—'

'Amy, you are not to say such things! You are not cross-grained! You are the kindest, brightest girl I have ever known, and I shall love you until all the cliffs at Bourne Bottom have tumbled into the sea and washed away.'

'Shall you, Jeffrey?' she said, suddenly shy. 'I hope so, because I shall love you for as long, and it would be so lonely without you.'

As he took her in his arms, she swayed towards him so that they were almost one. The Indian shawl slipped from her shoulders to make a little swathe of exotic colour in the grass, unnoticed. The sunlight gilded his hair and she let her hand wander over it as they kissed, loving the soft feel under her palm.

'My fortune-hunter,' she murmured with a little smile in her voice.

'You were all the fortune I ever wanted, dearest treasure,' he said. 'You know, of course, that I have no money worth speaking of. All the world will say I snared you for your inheritance.'

'Oh, let them,' she said dreamily. 'Let them. We'll be so happy, Jeffrey, that we won't care what anyone says.'

She was foretelling their future, she was sure. They would be happy. They had been through so much together and learned so much about each other that they were certain of their love. They had each other —there was nothing more in the world to ask for.